MW00811265

NEVER A SURE THING

Millie Curtis

Millie Curtis

Avid Readers Publishing Group
Lakewood, California

Avid Readers Publishing Group

http://www.avidreaderspg.com

ISBN-13: 978-1-61286-304-7

Printed in the United States

Dedication

For my loving parents Ray and Mildred Wilson. They believed in honesty, caring, and hard work. Thanks Mom and Dad for teaching us that life doesn't owe anyone a free ride.

Acknowledgements

Many thanks to proofreaders: Fred Curtis, Paige Lineweaver, Brooke Marker, Catherine Owens. If there remain a couple of typos, it is because I am the in-between from corrections to the publisher.

Praise to Elizabeth Curtis Blye, who is my stand-by computer rescuer and photographer.

Applause for Anica Moran. Where would I be without my lovely granddaughter who never complains when I snag her for a model for my book covers?

And, thanks to Eric Patterson of Avid Readers Publishing Group who seems to have more patience than I.

CHAPTER 1

The bong of the grandfather clock striking one o'clock in the afternoon caused Adelaide Richards to breathe a heavy sigh of relief. Today is her last day at the Gibbs Secretarial Training School for Women. Behind her is one solid year of training, without one day of vacation, allowing her to receive a piece of paper declaring that she is a proper, certified, bona fide secretary and bookkeeper, unusual for women of her day.

Adelaide had been a good student. She mastered Business English, Business Math, Typewriting and Stenography. Hours were spent learning the ins and outs of a Royal typewriter. She was a whiz at cleaning, oiling, changing ribbon, and unsticking stuck keys. Adelaide could even make carbon copies without getting ink on her fingers or smudges on the paper. Writing in shorthand was also a challenge. It was like learning a foreign language or writing in code. Adelaide attacked the course with a vengeance and used the new skill as often as possible.

Weekends and holidays had been spent learning propriety: proper table settings, proper table manners, proper behavior in public, and proper methods of greeting important people. It wasn't that everyone wasn't important, but many of the fifteen girls in her class were going to have prominent positions in government offices and notable corporations. Propriety in all manners of conduct was the maxim in 1917.

The school is housed in a huge Victorian house near Washington, D.C. The classrooms, kitchen and dining area, and administration offices are on the first floor. Students and two faculty members are housed upstairs. Most student rooms are shared, but Adelaide's roommate was one of the girls who had left, so she remained the sole occupant. That was fine with Adelaide.

After a tea reception, the girls are to be transported by bus to the Alexandria Union Train Station where they will go their separate ways. Some of the young ladies formed close friendships and are sad at the thought of parting. Adelaide had been friendly, but she put her energy into studies. Her bond with the rest of the girls was easy to sever. They had endured the training and now it was time to begin a new direction in their lives.

The year was already changing. Adelaide turned twenty in April, the same month President Wilson made a Declaration of War against Germany. The war had been raging in Europe for three years. Now America was drawn into it, causing apprehension among the public for what would happen next.

Adelaide was less concerned because she knew where she was going. She was going home. Not back to the tenant house where she had grown up, but to a large estate. Alexander Lockwood, the owner, had prepared a section of the house for her. She had spent two weeks there before entering the secretarial training school. Best of all, she was happy at the thought of being reunited with her best friend, Lottie Bell, who lived on the big farm.

Adelaide was in her room where she finished packing her belongings. She looked in the mirror to be sure her brown straw hat was pinned on correctly. She smoothed her plain traveling dress and laid a beige cotton shawl across her arm. The worker at the school was to load her satchel and suitcase into the bus. One more glance at her honey-colored bobbed hair, a smoothing of each eyebrow with her finger, a quick pass with a powder puff over her attractive face and she was ready.

She answered a knock at her door.

"I come to get your bags."

"Just the satchel and suitcase," Adelaide replied as she pointed to the articles on the bed. She didn't care for Willy, the man who worked around the school. She did her best to stay out of his path. He never gave her cause for concern but there was something about the weasel of a man that made her flesh crawl. Some girls said they caught him trying to peer through the transom window in the bathroom causing them to fashion cardboard to fit the window. No creepy peeping Toms allowed.

Adelaide left her room. When she reached the gathering room she was escorted to a designated chair by one of the teachers. After Adelaide took her seat, she looked about the large room. It was an impressive reception area and lavishly furnished in contrast to the rest of the rooms in the building. Royal blue velvet drapes trimmed in gold cordage hung at two long windows. The elongated tea and buffet table was covered by a pure white linen tablecloth. Trays of finger sandwiches, tiers of scones and delicate desserts were carefully placed on bone-white china platters atop the cloth. A vase of red roses, used as the centerpiece, drew her eye. How simple and elegant. Tea was set up at both ends of the table where two faculty members had been given the honor of pouring for the new graduates.

After a greeting by the head of the school and an invocation by another faculty member, awards were presented of which Adelaide received one for her academic performance. Then the director gave a short speech and handed out the diplomas. Once the mundane ceremonies were finished, Adelaide was eager to be on her way. Until everyone else was ready to go she was stuck, so she endured the tea and refreshments doing her best not to tap her feet or drum her fingers on the arm of the chair.

Adelaide was joining the line of young ladies boarding the bus when one of the teachers came to her side, her voice confidential. "Miss Richards, you have been one of our most promising students. Are you sure you are making the right decision to return home? Opportunities are opening up for women. You could do well if you stay in the city."

That possibility had already occurred to Adelaide. "Thank you for the compliment, Miss Stevens. I don't regret my decision."

"If circumstances change, please let me know. I have favorable contacts. You can reach me here at the school."

Adelaide smiled. "That's very kind. Thank you." But she didn't take the advice to heart.

As the gears shifted and the seats shook, the bus rattled away. Addie smiled to herself. She knew what was waiting for her: the farm, Lottie, and the promise of what lay ahead.

CHAPTER 2

Alexander Lockwood rolled up the shade on his apartment window overlooking Main Street in Berryville, Virginia. The sun was shining on this last day of May. Alex owned this building that housed his law office below. The building was tucked between two other establishments in the small town that served as the county seat of Clarke County, Virginia.

His plans were to close out his law practice and rent the building once he saw his farm, north of town, was on solid footing.

Alex had been a successful lawyer in Richmond and Washington before returning to his boyhood roots. His parents were getting on in years and the big place they owned would pass on to his brothers. At thirty-six, it was time to get on with life as he envisioned it, and the compelling reason he bought his own estate.

He dressed in a hurry because he was a few minutes behind schedule. Breakfast and dinner were eaten at the Battletown Inn. He never had time for lunch. He always wrapped up a piece of buttered bread in waxed paper and stuck it into his coat pocket, just in case. The birds were getting fat on buttered bread crumbs.

Alex checked to be sure his pocket watch was in place in the vest of his three-piece suit and placed his boater straw hat on his head before he went down the stairs. With a jaunty step, he headed out on this spirit-lifting day. Adelaide was returning and he was going to surprise her by meeting her at the Bluemont train station.

Alex had loaned her money for the cost of her training because he wanted to be sure she was capable of handling the secretarial affairs related to the farm. Now he would reap the rewards of his investment.

Adelaide grew up in a tenant house on his father's estate, but Alex only met her once when his brother, Clayton, introduced her. Adelaide and her friend, Lottie, had taken off on an adventure to Colorado a few months later. While there they became concerned their landlady was being coerced into turning over her affairs to another boarder. Adelaide called Alex for his advice because she knew he was a lawyer and had been a quixotic interest of her mother's when her mother was fifteen.

Why Alex felt he owed Adelaide something when she telephoned, he wasn't quite sure. He was scheduled to address the Colorado Bar so why not help Addie out. She was a young girl adrift in a strange place and could use sound advice. That was almost two years ago and the thought made him smile.

It was in Leadville he met Addie's friend, Lottie Bell Foster, and an Oklahoma cowboy, Caleb Dunn. Caleb and Lottie married and now live on Alex's farm where Caleb took the position of foreman. Lottie seemed to be enjoying her life as a married woman.

Alex had made the trip to Leadville twice. The first time was to make a smooth financial path for Adelaide's landlady in case her health deteriorated. The second time was a couple weeks later when Lottie was on what could have been her deathbed with pneumonia.

Was it Providence that set the wheels in motion? The Leadville trips wiped the cobwebs from his eyes about the direction of his life. It was in Leadville Alex decided to go off on the venture of giving up law for farming.

Now, Addie was coming home. They had not seen each other for a year. There had been no romantic attachment between them, but Alex knew he held deep feelings for Adelaide. He tried to toss his feelings aside because there was that age difference of sixteen years.

He greeted Henry, the boy who worked at the inn. "How are things with you today, Henry?"

"Right good so far," he replied. "How are things with you, Mr. Lockwood?"

"Looking up," answered Alex as he gave Henry a pat on the shoulder.

Alex had taken a copy of the *Clarke Courier* with him to read during breakfast. Whatever the news was in the county he hoped he wasn't a part of it. The editor's wife, Lavinia Talley, was the bloodhound in town. If there was a story brewing, her nose was right on it to carry it forward, whether she got the facts right or not.

The big news for the past few months had been about being drawn into World War I. Some troops had been sent and the military was gearing up. The war was bound to affect him in some way; Alex wasn't sure how.

After breakfast he went to his office. His plan was to work until three-thirty because Addie's train was scheduled to arrive at four-thirty and he wanted to be up on the mountain to meet it. He shuffled the papers on his desk. There were three cases that needed his attention: a juvenile charged with destruction of property, an irascible local charged for being drunk and disorderly, an elderly woman trying to pull her affairs in order after the untimely death of her husband. If Alex had a choice, he wouldn't get involved with any of them, but the destruction of property was coming before the judge next week so he, begrudgingly, pulled the case before him.

When the clock on the wall struck on the half-hour, Alex cleared up the desk, took his hat from a peg, locked the front door and left by the back, locking the door on his way out.

His 1915 Franklin touring car, transported four-hundred miles from the factory in Syracuse, New York, was parked behind his building. The auto was an extravagance, unusual for Alex. His reasons for purchasing the luxury car three months ago were because it had six cylinders and could travel twenty-five miles per hour, plus, it would go forty-six miles on a gallon of gasoline. It was also less expensive than the new models that were coming out. The car had a green body and black canvas top, spoke wheels, side mirrors and a black running board. It was comfortable and quietly impressive. Although Alex was not a big man, he felt a head taller driving the 1915 Franklin touring car.

CHAPTER 3

After the car climbed the mountain road, Alex pulled the auto to the side of the hard-packed, wide, dirt lane that led to the small Bluemont train station. He was early. He took his time walking to the station where he sat under a tree allowing him a good view of passengers alighting the train. Please let them all be strangers, he thought. He had no interest in answering questions as to why he was there.

The train was on time and came to a stop. Passengers left the railcars before it continued to the roundabout heading the train back east.

A quick pang of pleasure shot through Alex when he spied Adelaide the minute she stepped onto the platform. She had changed. Her appearance was as appealing as he remembered, and it wasn't only the new hairstyle, which was attractive, Adelaide Richards had attained a self-confidence in her carriage that caught his eye. Leaving his spot under the tree he went to meet her.

She was bending over to pick up her suitcase when he reached for the handle. "Hello, Addie."

She turned in surprise. "Alex! How did you know I was coming?"

"I called the school. I thought it would be better for me to drive you to the farm. It didn't occur to me until just now that you might want to go to your parents' house first."

"No. I want to get settled. I'm pleased you came. I was dreading having to ride in that car Mr. Marks uses to transport people." She was trying to sound nonchalant. The presence of Alex had sent a warm rush and she hoped he didn't notice the rosy flush she could feel in her face.

Alex carried her suitcase and satchel to his waiting car.

Addie stopped in her tracks. "Alex. What a beautiful car."

"It will last me a good long time," he responded. He held open the door of the passenger's side for Addie to enter and placed her belongings in the back seat.

"It is so good to be home," she said. "I do thank you for sending me to school. I learned so much more than I expected, although it was long and hair-pulling at times. I'm glad it's over. I did well in my studies."

He took his place behind the wheel and smiled over at her. "I knew you would." Alex pulled the throttle, turned the key in the ignition, released his foot from the clutch and they were headed out of the small hamlet of Bluemont. The auto made its way down the curvy mountain road into the village of Pine Grove, across the Shenandoah River Bridge, and they went west toward Berryville.

"What has changed?" she asked. "I feel as though I've been in a cloistered nunnery."

He laughed and his warm brown eyes twinkled. "What do you know about a cloistered nunnery?"

She chuckled. "I've read about them."

"Nothing much has changed in Berryville. Mrs. Talley keeps us all informed." Alex glanced over at her. "Talk is one thing that hasn't changed. That's why I am taking the back road to the farm rather than drive into town. I still have my law practice. I believe discretion is the wiser path to take."

Addie sighed. "I'm just happy to be back. I can hardly wait to see Lottie. How are she and Caleb doing?"

Alex turned onto a side dirt road. "Fine as far as I know. I don't see much of Lottie except to wave, if she's out. Caleb is doing a good job of building up my stock."

Addie's heart was beating like a drum. Just this small talk between them when all she wanted to say was how overjoyed she was to be sitting next to him. He once signed a note, "I send my love". Had she misjudged his feelings toward her? Was she a silly dreamer? No, she was a bright young woman who could keep her emotions in check.

Addie thought Alex had changed. Where was the carefree spirit she had seen in him when they were in Colorado? There wasn't a sign of it. And, they weren't in Colorado. They were back home where everyone did their best to be on guard lest their actions would be misinterpreted.

13

In a cheerful voice, she asked, "Have you heard from Clayton?"

Alex hesitated. "Have you?"

His response miffed Adelaide. "You know I haven't been allowed any correspondence except from immediate family for one long year. Rules of the school if you recall."

"Sorry. I forgot. Clay will be returning next week from the university, so I have been informed."

"You don't sound over-enthused."

"Even though he is my brother, I hardly know him. There are too many years between us. You know Clay better than I do. We had a talk while you were in Colorado. I believe he is quite taken with you, Adelaide." He looked over at her.

Her response was firm. "I wrote to him before I left Leadville and told him I had no intentions toward him. Clay and I had a lot of fun when we were young and growing up on your father's place."

He shrugged a shoulder. "I understood that. He needs to get serious about what he wants to do with his life. He can't be hanging onto father's coattails forever."

Those words did not please Adelaide. "That isn't fair. I believe he has one more year at Charlottesville before he settles into whatever he wants to do. You had that luxury if I'm not mistaken." Her attractive face held a determined look.

"I like a woman who speaks her mind." He grinned. "It's good to have you back, Addie."

The road they were on met the Charles Town Pike. Alex turned and traveled south. She looked up and saw the majestic white house on a hill in the distance. He turned right onto the road that led up to the farm. Two more sharp curves and then a right turn onto the drive of his place.

Addie looked at the sign posted. *Lockwood.* "I see you have named the place after yourself. That's not very original."

He smiled over at her. "I want people to know where I live."

The two-story, white stucco house sat perched on a hill overlooking the vast acres that comprised the place. Limestone steps led up to a wide porch with tall white columns.

Addie gazed in wonder as they drove up the drive. In the hollow, she saw the brick house where Lottie and Caleb lived. Cattle, sheep, goats, horses and chickens all seemed to have their places. Land had been plowed and freshly sown and crops were beginning to pop up through the soil. The place felt alive.

Addie thought of the two weeks she had spent here before she'd gone to school. Except for the times she had visited with Lottie, she had welcome solitude. She liked her quiet times. Alex had not come to the farm until the day she left for school. He stayed in his apartment in town. Now she had returned and she warmed to the sense of being home. Life held the promise and anticipation for what lay ahead. Will she be disappointed?

CHAPTER 4

Alex parked in front of the house and removed her bags from the car. Addie went on ahead up the steps and waited for him to open the tall door.

"Ella should be around someplace," he said.

"Ella?"

"I had to hire a new maid to take care of the house."

"It is a big house for one person to care for," Addie remarked.

"As the place begins to pay for itself, I can hire more help. The only room used upstairs is the one I sleep in when I come, so it is just the downstairs she needs to be concerned about."

Adelaide unpinned her hat. "How often do you come?"

"I try to make it every weekend. Sometimes I am pressed for time and have to miss. With you here, you can straighten out the bookwork and take that burden from me." His smile was apologetic. "I'm afraid the books are not in the best shape."

Addie brightened. "That's what I'm here for, and I am all for getting down to business tomorrow, once I go to see Lottie."

"I'm sure she will be pleased to see you."

The house had a wide central foyer with a circular staircase that led up to the second floor. The office and Addie's quarters were to the left. Under the stairs was a large closeted area for storage of articles. To the right of the foyer was the parlor and behind that the dining room and kitchen. All rooms had high ceilings and a stone fireplace except the maid's, which was a smaller room off the kitchen.

Adelaide held her hat in her hand. "I'll put my things in my room and then we can check the office," she said.

Alex smiled at her. "I'll carry your bags in and then hunt up the maid. I can use something to eat."

At that moment there was a creaking of a door and a pretty young girl came into the hall. "I thought I heard voices. I got dinner ready for you, Mister Alex."

"Addie, this is Ella." To the maid, he said, "This is Miss Richards. I told you she would be coming here to work as my secretary."

The maid gave a slight curtsy, "I'm right pleased to meet you, ma'am."

"Thank you, Ella. I'm happy to be here."

The maid wasn't much younger than Adelaide, and a comely young woman at that. Perhaps that was a better situation than to have an older woman who would try to order her around. Still, Addie would rather the maid was on the homely side.

"Put another place at the table for Miss Richards," ordered Alex. "I will spend the night here, so you can prepare my room."

"Yes, Mister Alex." And, away went Ella to do his bidding.

"She's not from around here," observed Adelaide.

"No, she's from North Carolina. Her family moved up near Winchester. A friend said she could use employment. Ella has been here for two weeks and I have no complaints to this point."

Addie headed toward her quarters. "You can leave my things in my sitting room. I'd like to freshen up before we eat."

He chuckled. "You're as good at giving orders as I am."

He was right. She had talked to him as she had to that weasel of a Willy at the training school. "Alex, I am so sorry. I didn't mean to sound bossy."

"You are forgiven. I'll see you in the dining room."

Addie went to the room she had used for two weeks before she had gone to school and found it as she had left it. From the long window she could see the Blue Ridge Mountains in the distance. They couldn't compare to the Rockies, but she loved them just the same. A ewer held lukewarm water. She poured some into the basin on the dry sink and washed her hands and face before she dabbed on toilet water. One look in the mirror to reset a strand of honey-colored hair and she was ready.

Alex pulled a chair from under the oak dining table for Addie. It was a comfort to be seated at the table with him, just the two of them.

"This is the most relaxed I've felt in a year," she remarked.

"I'm glad," he said. "When I want to relax, I think of Caleb's camp up in Leadville. Remember how peaceful that was, Addie?"

A longing smile appeared on her face. "I do. That was almost two years ago. Sometimes it feels like yesterday and at other times it seems like forever. If I close my eyes, I can picture the small waterfall and the beautiful mountains capped with snow."

He laughed. "And Momma Cat depositing her two kittens in the corner of the cabin."

Addie joined in his laughter. "That was something, wasn't it?"

The maid came into the room with a beef roast ringed with vegetables. Addie had forgotten how hungry she was until the aroma filled her senses. "Ella this looks and smells delicious."

"My ma was a good cook. I baked apple dumplins' for dessert."

A good cook, perhaps, but Adelaide would have to teach Ella about proper table settings and serving manners. Addie smiled to herself. Gibbs Secretarial Training School had left its mark.

After dinner was over, the sun had set. Alex said, "Let's leave the office until the morning. I've had a busy week. A full night's sleep will be welcome."

Addie yawned. "I have to agree. What an exciting day this has been!"

Alex looked directly at her. "The most exciting part is having you back. It has been a long year."

Far too long, thought Addie. She smiled back at him. "Good night, Alex. I will meet you first thing in the morning."

CHAPTER 5

Addie awoke early. It was the odor of brewed coffee and frying bacon that caused her to stir from a deep sleep. At first she thought she was back home in the tenant house. The sun, peeking through the cracks in the shutters, brought her to life. She left the oak bed and smoothed the sheets before pulling up the patchwork quilt covered with squared material of roses and delicate flowers. She opened the shutters and took in the scene of the vast estate. It was going to be a lovely day.

Addie hurried to get ready and took her clothes from a small closet in the room, where she had hung her slim wardrobe, and determined she needed to buy a new hat and dress. Well, a new hat, anyway. She wasn't sure how much money she would earn. It was something she and Alex hadn't discussed. What if he expected her to work for free until she had paid back the cost of schooling? That possibility was not a pleasant thought.

Addie took a white waist and copper colored skirt from the closet and dressed in a hurry. She wore brown cotton knee-high stockings and tied the laces in her plain brown leather shoes. Special care was taken with combing her bobbed hair and applying a hint of rouge to her cheeks. She wanted to look her best to meet Alex.

Addie went into the dining room. He was seated and rose when she entered.

A white shirt and linen trousers complemented his lean frame. "You look bright and cheerful," he greeted her. "Did you sleep well?"

"Very well, thank you."

He pulled out a chair for her. "Ella has breakfast for us and then we can get started on the task at hand."

"I do want to visit Lottie."

He nodded as he returned to his chair. "I know. We can work for a couple of hours and take a break."

Addie looked over at him. His short brown hair was neatly combed and parted on the side. He wasn't handsome but his angular face came alive when he smiled. Addie had kept company with Alex enough to know that it was his brown eyes that revealed his inner emotions. Right now they were looking at her.

Addie cleared her throat, picked up a platter and placed scrambled eggs on her plate. They had eaten together many times. Why did she feel embarrassed this morning?

Alex didn't seem to notice. He was busy devouring eggs, bacon, and a biscuit in gravy. He glanced up. "Better eat more than that. You've got a long day ahead of you."

A smile was her reply as she put a piece of bacon on her plate.

Once breakfast was finished they went into the office, which was in disarray. "I've tried to keep the expenditures and income separate," he informed her. "That pile has to do with horses, that one's for cattle, then there's the rest of it."

The appearance of the office caused Addie to take a deep breath. She wasn't sure what she had expected, but she hadn't expected one year of paperwork to be strewn about. No wonder Alex didn't want to tackle it last night.

"What is that pile?" asked Addie, pointing to a heap of papers on the windowsill.

"That's the payroll. Caleb's hired three men and I have to pay Ella."

The time was perfect for her to say, "We haven't discussed how I am to repay you for the cost of my schooling."

"That isn't something we need to talk about right now," he answered.

"But it is," she countered. "Our agreement was that I would work in repayment, which I plan to do. I need to know what you expect."

Alex became all business. "Then we will make out a contract. I will pay you thirty dollars a month in wages, and you will pay me ten dollars a month for the next ten months."

Addie did a quick calculation in her head. "That means the tuition was one hundred dollars. Do you have a receipt?"

Adelaide Richards could be irksome.

"Yes, I have a receipt. Don't be so hard-nosed, Addie."

"I'm sorry if I sound that way. If I learned anything at that school, I learned to make sure everything balances."

With a healthy yank, Alex pulled out the desk chair, took a seat, rummaged around for a sheet of clean paper and jabbed a pen in the inkwell. "I'll put the contract in writing!"

"Would you like to have me type it? I'll use a sheet of carbon paper and make a copy for each of us."

Alex laid the pen on an ink blotter. He crossed his arms and looked at her. "I'm almost sorry for sending you to school. I'm not sure there is any carbon paper here."

"You had your secretary in town buy office supplies, remember? It's in the bottom left-hand drawer. At least it was there when I left last year, and it doesn't look to me as though that drawer has been disturbed."

The drawer had been difficult to open but Addie had found a way to wiggle it just right. She couldn't suppress a chuckle when she found the carbon in its sealed box. "Move over, Alex, and I'll show you how well your investment has turned out."

He laughed as he stood up and offered her his chair. "Do you think we are going to be able to work together?"

She sent a playful look. "As long as you bring the information and allow me to file it in its place, I don't see why not."

He sat on the edge of the desk and watched as she prepared to type. "Perhaps you can handle my law practice, too."

Her eyes were on her task. "Don't you have straight-laced Jane to take care of you?"

"Yes, but she's only there two days a week and not nearly as much fun to watch."

Addie moved the carriage of the typewriter. "Careful, Alex. You may cause me to make a mistake."

He got up from the desk with a satisfied smile. "I'll dig into that pile on the windowsill first."

A hint of the carefree Alex had returned. Addie breathed an inner sigh of relief.

CHAPTER 6

Two hours later, Addie was walking to Lottie's house. It had been so long since she had taken a walk in the quiet of the country that she felt like skipping, a desire she hadn't experienced since she was a little girl.

Lottie was hanging wash on the clothesline. When she heard Adelaide call, she dropped the wet towel she was holding and ran to meet her. They hugged as tightly as bark clings to the trunk of a tree.

"Addie, I can't believe you're here." And Lottie Bell, who was not one to show her emotions, had tears running down her cheeks. "Lord, you don't know how happy I am to see you."

"I hope those are tears of joy," said Adelaide. "I am glad to be back."

Lottie wiped her face with her apron. "Come inside. It's lunchtime. I'll fix some tea and sandwiches," she offered. "We have so much to talk about."

"A grand idea," answered Addie. "I'll finish hanging your laundry while you rustle up the grub." She snickered at her words. "Isn't that what Caleb would say?"

Lottie laughed. "He would. The clothespins are in the bag," she advised. "Hurry up because I am dying to catch up on all the news."

Addie felt welcome the minute she stepped inside the bungalow. The house had a living room, dining room and kitchen with stairs leading up to three bedrooms. Alex had said it was a nice house and it was.

"Go ahead upstairs," Lottie called. "You've got a few minutes before I get this on the table."

Addie went up the stairs. She could see Lottie had been busy making this little house a home. Addie smiled when she spotted a patchwork quilt made with the extra material Leopold Goldman had given to Lottie when she worked at the Golden Eagle Department Store in Leadville. Memories of the time they had spent in Colorado were popping up all over.

Lottie called from the bottom of the stairs, "Soup's on."

Addie laughed aloud as she came down the stairs. "You sound like Mrs. Tygert. Weren't we lucky to land at her boarding house?"

Lottie agreed. "I think of her often and wonder if her boarder, Tilly Stiles, has changed any."

Addie took a seat at the dining room table where Lottie had placed chicken salad sandwiches made with bread she had baked the day before.

Lottie poured tea and sat her plump body opposite Adelaide. The room was cozy.

"Tell me about Caleb. Is he satisfied to have taken this job?" asked Adelaide.

"He says he is. I don't see as much of him as I'd like to."

Addie put half a sandwich on her plate and took a sip of tea. "Alex tells me Caleb has hired three more men."

Lottie nodded. "One of them is his friend, Jess."

"Jess?" Addie questioned.

"He's the one who went into partnership with Caleb when they were going to strike it rich in gold."

Recognition came to the visitor. "I remember Caleb saying that. And Jess decided he liked cattle better than digging for gold so he went back to Oklahoma." Addie asked, "What is he like?"

Lottie shrugged a shoulder. "He's good looking and Caleb says he's a good worker, but…"

Addie looked over at her friend. "But, what?"

"Caleb spends more time with him than he does with me."

"You don't approve?"

Lottie was indignant. "Of course I don't."

Addie winced. "How long has Jess been here?"

"Since April. Caleb says he wants to help Jess settle in and feel comfortable. This area is a lot different from Oklahoma."

Addie smiled. "Lottie Bell, I think you're jealous."

"I am not!" she retorted. Then a sly smile creased her face. "Well, maybe I am. I like to have Caleb around and he puts in long hours."

Addie smiled back at her friend. "Once this place is on solid footing, I'm sure he will have more time to devote to you."

"I know you're right. It can get lonesome out here. Tell me about your year at school. Are you glad you went?"

Addie held her teacup and sat back in the chair. "It was a hard year. I learned a lot and acquired skills I will be able to use in any office. One of the teachers suggested that I would do better to stay in Washington. I did think about it, Lottie. You know I like to see what is on the other side of the hill."

Lottie raised an eyebrow. "But you owed Alex. How do you feel about him?"

Addie hesitated. "I'm not sure. I was so happy to get back here. He's different than when we were in Colorado. I know he's pleased that I'm here, but he is strictly business."

"He has to be cautious. You know how it is."

Addie agreed. "I know how it is. I have a lot to straighten out as far as the farm is concerned and I am looking forward to being busy. I don't like to sit still too long."

"That's one thing about you that hasn't changed," said Lottie.

Addie looked up in surprise. "Do you think I've changed?"

"I think you've grown for the better. You are more upright and stylish. I like your hair. I have not been brave enough to cut mine."

"The school was big as to how we appeared to the public. I wasn't aware that it showed."

Lottie smiled an approving smile. "Let it show. We have always looked at life from a different angle. I am living my dream. You haven't found yours."

Addie sat up straight. "I don't want to change. I want us to always be close."

"That will never be any different," advised a wise Lottie. "There is a connection between us that can't be broken no matter what life throws in our way. Now, how would you like some applesauce cookies?"

Addie laughed, "You and cookies. I know that is one connection that will never be severed."

They ate the cookies while reminiscing.

"You have dressed this house up," said an appreciative Adelaide.

"I've helped Miss Butler out a few times and she gives me scrap material from the dress shop that I've been able to use."

"Miss Butler?" said Addie. "The woman who always looks like she has eaten a sour pickle."

Lottie chuckled.

Addie continued, "I want to buy a new dress and hat once I earn some money. I'm still wearing the hats I bought from Miss Ramsburg before we went to Colorado."

Lottie informed. "She's not Miss Ramsburg anymore. She married that man from Washington. Then some newcomer bought the hat shop. Now that young woman is married and the millinery has been closed for a couple of months."

This was unwelcome news. "I'm sorry to hear that, but I am pleased for Miss Ramsburg."

"Mrs. Burke," interjected Lottie.

"Maybe the shop will be open when I can afford a hat. Right now, I own fifty cents. Alex picked me up at the train station or I would have had to pay my last cent to ride in with Herbert Marks."

Lottie was still thinking of the millinery. "I wish Mary Lee Graves could afford to own that shop."

"I don't know Mary Lee Graves," said Addie.

"Sure you do. She was a Thompson and used to help Miss Catherine. Miss Butler gives her work when there's a big doings. Mary Lee could fashion a hat for you."

"I wish I could have bought one in Mr. Goldman's store."

And then they got reminiscing about their days in Leadville; laughing until their sides hurt.

When Lottie could talk, she said, "Addie, I told you we would have a great tale to tell our grandchildren."

Adelaide agreed. "I am so glad we went." After a moment of hesitation she changed the subject. "Lottie, I plan on going to visit my family on Friday. Do you want to go?"

"Will we be back in time for dinner? I like to give Caleb a good meal."

"I'll take the buggy. We can leave at eight o'clock and be back in the afternoon."

Lottie was all for it. "I haven't seen my mother for over a month."

"It'll be fun. Just you and me without a care in the world," came Addie's enthusiastic reply. "Now, I've got to get back to finish what I started by sorting out the mess in the bookkeeping."

They walked to the door together and hugged before Adelaide left. Lottie waved at her friend and watched as Addie went back through the fields to the big white house that sat on the hill.

CHAPTER 7

When Addie arrived, she found Alex had left. That was fine with her because she had a lot of work to do and she preferred to work alone. With four hours of good daylight left, she wanted to make the most of them.

The maid stopped by the open office door. "Miss Richards, Mister Alex told me to tell you that he would come back sometime Saturday. Do you want I should make dinner?"

"Please call me Adelaide. No thank you, Ella. I had a good lunch. If I get hungry, I'll find something." Addie should have stopped there but she couldn't help herself. "Do you like Mister Alex?"

"Yes, ma'am. I surely do. He's right nice to work for. I jus' love bein' here."

Addie eyed the pretty lithe girl standing before her with shiny raven hair and dark eyes. "How old are you, Ella?"

"Sixteen."

"I'm glad you're here."

Ella gave a slight nod. "Thank you, ma'am. Mister Alex said that I should get you whatever you need."

"That's very kind," replied Addie. "I believe I am set for the night."

"Yes, ma'am," and away went Ella.

33

Adelaide Richards smiled to herself. Sixteen and lacking in education, Ella was no threat.

The pile of papers on the windowsill had been properly filed before she left for Lottie's. How would she tackle the rest? She began with the horses because she figured they would be the biggest headache: where they were bought, how much they cost, what was their lineage, how many had been sold and to whom. It would require careful record keeping.

With a heavy sigh, Addie looked at the other piles. Luck had to be on her side to get them finished tomorrow. The next day she and Lottie were going to visit their parents and Adelaide wanted everything in order when Alex returned on Saturday. She felt the need to prove to him that she was capable.

By the time the sun set, Addie had finished her work. She stretched to loosen up her tired body and went to the kitchen for a cup of tea.

With cup in hand, she walked out onto the front porch and sat in a rocker where she could overlook the countryside. The sun was setting and the air was cooler. The only sound was the high chirping of the tree frogs. In the distance she could hear the sound of the train as it traveled north bringing a reminiscent sigh. She knew where the passengers were headed. Off to Martinsburg and Hagerstown, two states away. She and Lottie had taken that same trip. Was it almost two years ago?

When dusk set in, Addie left her chair and went inside to get ready for bed. Tomorrow would be a full day of work and she wanted to be rested.

She threw the soft cotton gown over her head before she washed up, then opened the window to allow the pleasant southwest breeze to waft through the room. It felt so good to climb into the waiting bed. An old house has its creaks and groans but Addie was so tired, she fell fast asleep.

**

The next morning she awoke to a blood-curdling scream. Grabbing her robe and wrapping it around, she flew out the back door barefooted.

Ella stood by the well, shaking and crying while wringing her hands in her apron.

"What is it?" shouted Addie as she ran toward her.

"A big ol' black snake, Miss Adelaide. I ain't never seen anythin' so big!" The maid was frozen in her spot.

"Where did it go?" asked Addie, eyeing the area around, afraid it might still be close.

"I ain't for sure an' I ain't lookin' for it. I was so scared. I jus' came to fill up the pail and out it slithered. Slimy ol' thing!"

Caleb arrived on the scene. "What happened?" Then he spied Adelaide and burst into a wide grin. "Addie! Lottie told me you were here. I have to say it's right nice to see you. What's goin' on here?"

"Hi, Caleb. Ella saw a big black snake that frightened her. She's not sure where it went."

"Probably crawled off into the field."

"I don't want it around the house," said Addie. "I don't like snakes any more than Ella does. You'd better have somebody cut this tall grass, find the snake and kill it, Caleb."

"I don't like to kill black snakes. They help get rid of vermin. He was most likely as afraid of you as you were of him."

"Maybe so, but I don't care what color they are or how much good they do, I don't want to find any surprising me around the house!"

The shock of her awakening was gone and Addie realized she was standing there in front of Caleb barefooted and in her light robe. She pulled the robe tighter and assumed a more dignified air. "Please excuse the way I look. How have you been, Caleb?"

"Gosh. Don't be so stiff, Addie."

"I'm embarrassed," she admitted.

A slow, sly smile appeared on his sun-touched, pleasant face. "You got no call to be. You look right fine."

"Caleb Dunn, you behave or I'm going to tell Lottie." Then she smiled. "Did she tell you that she and I are going to visit our parents tomorrow?"

"Did Lottie tell me? She ordered me to have the buggy ready by eight o'clock sharp. Sometimes she gets lonesome out here. I suppose I ain't around as much as I should be, but seein' you're back it's goin' to be easier on her."

Addie touched his hand. "It's going to be good for both of us," she replied.

Then she turned to the young girl whose icy scream had awakened her. "Are you feeling all right now?"

In a shaky voice, Ella answered. "I 'spect I'll get over it. You want eggs for breakfast?"

The crisis had passed. "That will be fine. How about you, Caleb? Want to join me for breakfast?"

"No thanks. Lottie always makes sure I get plenty to eat." He tipped the brim of his big western hat. "Seein' you ladies have recovered, I'll be on my way. Plenty of work ahead of me."

Addie put her arm around Ella's shoulders. "I'll get dressed while you prepare breakfast. I have a lot of work ahead of me, also."

The snake was forgotten, but the shaken pair kept a wary eye as they made their way back to the house.

CHAPTER 8

Friday looked to be another warm June day. One more glance around the office and Addie felt rewarded that her diligence had paid off. Alex would find the room neat and orderly when he arrives tomorrow.

Caleb had the horse hitched to a two-wheel buggy and Lottie was in the driver's seat when Addie went out the front door.

She waved as Addie hurried down the stone steps. "Do you want me to drive?"

"You drive over and I'll drive back."

"That's fair," agreed Lottie. "My arms get tired."

Lottie chucked to the horse and they were on their way.

It was five miles to town and Addie was eager to see if it had changed. She wanted to go into Irene Butler's dress shop, Mr. White's general store, and the millinery. But, Lottie had said the hat shop was closed and Addie had no money, so they would just have to ride through the town and take in the sights.

Secretly, she hoped Alex wouldn't see them ride by his law office. Why this bothered Adelaide, she didn't know. Perhaps she felt guilty being away from the farm. She knew that the office affairs of the farm were in good shape. What if Alex expected her to be there at all times unless she asked permission first?

A little voice reminded her that she was not in school anymore. She was a twenty-year-old woman capable of making her own decisions. Her allegiance to Alexander Lockwood was to keep the records straight. So, if he espied them riding by, there was no cause for alarm. How easily she could resolve her doubts.

At the Hawthorne House in town, Lottie turned left onto the main street of Berryville. Addie watched as they drove the two blocks that comprised the town. If there was a difference, it had to be the presence of a few cars parked on the street.

The barber shop, the hotel and Coyner's department store appeared the same. The hat shop looked forlorn with the closed sign hung in the window.

"I can't understand how someone can own that shop and not keep it open," Addie commented to Lottie.

"I heard that the young woman who bought it married one of the well-to-do from the southern end of the county," Lottie replied.

Addie gave a sideways glance. "That doesn't explain why the shop isn't open."

"What do you think?" answered Lottie. "Money is not a concern. The couple lives in Washington. Does that explain it?"

Addie ignored her friend's explanation. "I wish I owned that place."

Lottie laughed, "What would you do with it? You don't even like to pick up a needle and thread."

Addie continued to view the shop as they passed by. "I'd hire you to make the hats and I would concentrate on the ready-made goods. Wouldn't it be great to own your own shop?"

"Adelaide Richards, you are a dreamer. Don't look now, but Ol' Miss Talley is peeking out her window. I see the lace curtains waver."

A moment of bedevilment snared Addie. She smiled and waved in that direction. "Lucky us. Maybe we'll make the weekly paper."

Lottie shook her head. "We're not newsworthy. Now, if she knew that you are living out at Lockwood and that Alex spends his weekends up there, a story worthy of the esteemed paper may be in order."

Addie playfully tapped her friend's shoulder. "Ooh, Lottie Bell. Your mind is wandering."

The buggy continued on through town, across the railroad tracks. They passed the mill, Bel Voi and Clermont estates, and turned left into the lane east of town that led to where their parents lived.

"Shall I drop you off?" asked Lottie.

"No. I'll drive and drop you off. I'm not sure how well I am going to be received."

"You said your mother had forgiven you for not going to become a teacher," said Lottie as she pulled the horse to a stop.

Addie got down. "I'm not sure her heart was in it. Then I chose to stay at Alex's farm instead of the tenant house when we returned from Colorado, which probably didn't set well. I wrote home a couple of times when I was at the secretarial school but there was no reply."

"Did you ask her to write?"

"Why should I do that? Wouldn't you think that she would write without me asking?" answered a disgruntled Adelaide.

"I'm not sure, Addie. Your mom keeps things close. Maybe she thought you didn't want to hear from her."

"I guess you could be right. But, I am a bit antsy about going home."

Addie started the horse once Lottie was firmly seated. After they went by the big house, Addie turned off the lane and stopped in front of Lottie's former home. Her mother was sitting in a porch rocker, mending. The minute she saw them coming she placed her chore aside and hurried to meet them as the buggy stopped.

"My goodness, what a surprise!" she exclaimed. She hugged Lottie while Addie climbed down from the seat. Then Mrs. Foster hugged her as if she were her own. "Look at you, Adelaide. You have blossomed. Just wait until your momma sees you; she'll be so happy."

Addie was still uncertain. "I hope you're right Mrs. Foster. It is nice to see you once again." She turned to her friend. "Lottie, we will need to leave around three."

Adelaide climbed back up into the buggy and headed for the tenant house over the rise.

Laura Richards was hoeing in her vegetable garden when she saw the buggy. Unsure of who it was, she waited for a clear view.

"Addie?"

"Hi, Momma. I'm back." She hopped down to the ground and stood, unsure.

Her mother leaned on the hoe. "I almost didn't recognize you with your hair all short."

"It's a new style."

Laura Richards put out her hand and Addie ran to her. "I have missed you, Adelaide," she said as the hoe fell away and she warmly hugged her eldest child.

Addie swallowed hard and fought back tears as words flowed out in a shaky voice. "I was afraid you might not want to see me again. When I came back from Colorado for those two weeks, I didn't want to come back here and stay in the loft, but I should have come to see you."

Her mother released her hold. "We knew where you were. Alex told us."

"What did you think?"

Laura hesitated. "In truth, I was let down. I thought you should have come back here. You're a good girl, Addie. As long as you remember who you are, you won't be disappointed. Come into the house. I want to hear about your training."

They entered the room that served as kitchen and living room. Laura removed her soiled apron and washed her hands. "Cup of tea?"

"I can fix it, Momma. You look tired."

Adelaide rushed to the stove before her mother could get there. The teakettle held warm water so Addie moved it to a hotter burner on the wood stove. Then she took two mugs from the cupboard. When she had some money, she vowed to buy her mother decent teacups.

Laura Richards took a seat at the table. "Stop fussing around. I have been wanting to hear about that school you went to."

Addie came and sat opposite her mother. "It was wonderful. I learned so much. Maybe not as much as I'd learn as a teacher, but Momma, you can be pleased that I will always be able to take care of myself."

"I just want you to be happy."

Addie looked over at her mother's work-worn hands and tired eyes. "I am happy. You would be pleased with the grades I earned. One of the teachers said I was one of the most promising students. She even suggested that I should consider the opportunities for women opening up in the city."

A satisfied smile appeared on Laura's face. "You were always a good student."

Addie brightened. "It was your pushing that did it. I'm grateful to you, Momma, although I didn't like it at the time."

"Your pa always said I was hard on you. Maybe I was, but I didn't want you to get trapped. That worried me. Your Aunt Lilly said you would do well and you have."

"Why didn't you write to me at the training school? I thought you were mad at me."

"I'm not big on letter writing and you didn't ask. Your letters were enough to let us know all was well."

At this Addie laughed aloud. "Oh, Momma, that's just what Lottie said. I should have asked."

Laura took a more serious tone. "I know Alex paid for your school. He told your father. He said you were going to pay him back by taking care of his farm affairs. We could have paid for your schooling and you wouldn't owe him anything."

"I know. I didn't want that money spent on me. Keep it for Chip."

Laura sighed. "I'm working hard to keep him in school. He's fourteen and wants to quit." A wistful smile appeared. "Chip's different than Charlie. Charlie's cut out for farming. Your pa and I agreed that Chip has to finish high school. Maybe he'll be my teacher."

Addie grinned. "If not, there is always Sarah Jane. Where is she?"

"Charlie took her for a ride in the wagon. She loves her big brother. Can you believe she's three?" Laura left her chair and took her mug to the sink.

"I won't forget that day I helped bring her into this world. Every time I think of it, I shiver."

Laura came to the table and picked up Addie's mug. "You were strong that day. Want to take a walk out and see if we can see your pa? He'll be disappointed if he knows you were here and you didn't go looking for him."

Addie nodded. "I have time. I told Lottie I would pick her up at three."

"I saw Lottie's mother the other day," said Laura. "It seems Lottie is doing fine and both the Fosters like Caleb. I only met him once." Laura looked at her daughter, almost as though she was seeing her for the first time. "You know, Adelaide, we never learned much about your time in Colorado. I don't think we ever talked of anything at all. We're going to have to do that one day."

Mother and daughter walked side by side out to the fields to find John Richards. Addie felt a sense of relief. Her mother seemed sincerely pleased to see her and treated her as a grown woman. On this beautiful June day in Virginia, she couldn't ask for more than that.

CHAPTER 9

Alex arrived around ten o'clock Saturday morning. Adelaide was in the office filing papers. The office door was open when he approached.

He looked around the orderly room and gave a low whistle. "Good morning," he said. "I can see you have been busy."

Addie was sitting at the desk and looked up as he entered. "Good morning. I have made headway," she replied. Placing her hand on a stack of papers on the desk, she looked puzzled. "I'm not sure what to do with these."

Alex came to the desk and flipped through the pile. "Looks like information that has to do with crops."

Did he think she was a numb-skull? She sent him a distasteful look. "I gathered that. There are receipts for wheat, corn, cotton, hay. How do you want me to account for them? Do you want to know to whom they were sold, yield per acre, how much the seed cost, what was kept for use on the farm…"

He interrupted. "How do you think it should be handled?"

His unexpected question caused Adelaide to change her demeanor. She shifted in her chair and assumed a more official air. "I have given this thought. I believe all aspects are important. Each crop should have a separate folder. The general ledger will give you a quick look at income and outlay, and a separate folder can break down the nitty-gritty."

"That's exactly the way I'd handle it," he said.

Addie smiled at him. "I'll bet you don't even know what your total production was last year."

Alex gave a light nod. "Aha, you have discovered the secret of the jumble of papers before you. They have been waiting for your capable system of order."

Addie smiled and shook her head. "I don't know how you knew if you were making money or losing it."

Alex took a seat in an armchair at the side of the desk. "You are probably right. I have got to get serious about the financial end if I am going to make this place pay for itself. So far, I have concentrated on building up stock. Caleb has done a good job on that end. And, I have the best horse breeder in the area coming by this afternoon to give me advice. Grain and crop production is next on the list."

"When is he due to arrive?" asked Adelaide.

Alex sat relaxed with one knee crossed over the other, his arms resting on the arms of the chair. "One o'clock. I want you on hand to take notes of our conversation. I expect he has a wealth of information and I won't be able to absorb all of it."

"You don't expect me to follow you around when you go out to the horses, do you?"

He chuckled. "No. I want you to capture the conversation when we come back here for discussion." Alex rose from the chair. "Keeping notes should put some of that shorthand you learned to good use." Once again he surveyed the well-organized room. "I'm pleased." He turned his attention to Addie. "I believe you are going to be an asset to this place. See you around one." Out he went.

An asset? The word made it clear to Adelaide that she was an investment. Well, she determined that Alexander Lockwood would get his money's worth!

At one o'clock sharp, Addie's office door was ajar when she heard a knock on the front door. She went to answer it and felt her jaw drop at the sight of the man standing before her. He was over six feet tall with a swirl of black hair showing under his driver's cap. Dark eyes smiled at her. His chiseled features were those of a Greek god.

He touched his cap. "Good afternoon. I am James Anderson here to see Mr. Lockwood."

Addie caught her breath and quickly closed her mouth.

James smiled as though he was used to that kind of a reception.

Acting composed, she said, "Mr. Lockwood is expecting you. Please come in and have a chair."

"Thank you for the offer. I'll wait out here. As you can see I'm dressed for the horses."

Never a Sure Thing

She could see all right, and did her best not
to stare. She quickly took in his wide shoulders,
trim waist, riding pants that accentuated his long
legs and leather boots up to his knees. "I'll tell Mr.
Lockwood you are here."

James stayed on the porch taking in the view
before him while Addie hurried to find Alex.

She found him finishing his lunch in the
dining room. "Your horse man is here. He's waiting
on the porch."

"Good," he answered. "When we return, are
you going to be more comfortable in the parlor or
in the office?"

Adelaide wasn't sure she was going to be
comfortable either place, but she chose the office
where she could sit in a corner with her stenographic
notebook poised and ready. She planned to look as
in-charge and proper as she was trained to be.

When the men returned, Addie was waiting.
As she had anticipated, Alex chose the chair at the
desk while James settled into the armchair. They
paid no attention to the quiet secretary as the talk
began in earnest about horses.

Their discussion lasted over an hour.
Addie took careful notes while listening to James
Anderson's mellow voice dispense his knowledge.
The world of horses took on a whole new meaning
for Addie.

When James had gone, Adelaide was
prepared to type up the notes.

Alex came into the room. "How do you
think it went?" he asked.

"He seems to know horses," she replied.

"That he does. He got his start in the cavalry." With a tilt to the side and a nod of his head, he added, "James is a clever fox. He married a woman with no prospects and inherited an estate."

Addie stopped what she was doing. "Is that supposed to be admirable? Why are you telling me this?"

"Because James is still popular with the young ladies. I expect he will make a few more trips out here. I thought you should know."

She rolled the typing paper into place and eyed him squarely. "I shall take your information under advisement lest I get swept away."

CHAPTER 10

By the beginning of August, Adelaide had established a routine that seemed to be working well. She rose between six and six-thirty, straightened her room, dressed for the day and went to the dining room for breakfast before starting work in the office at eight.

Ella prepared Addie's meals. It was like living at the rooming house in Colorado where Mrs. Tygert prepared breakfast and dinner for her, Lottie, and Tilly Stiles. The difference was that Addie was eating alone in the large dining room and she didn't like the feeling. She missed having others around. Always there had been other people: the tenant house, the boarding house, the training school. She felt she was acting like the "lady of the manor", which she wasn't.

Readying the bookkeeping affairs had been time-consuming. In addition, there were letters to write, inquiries to answer, monthly pay for the hired help, herself included. Alex came on the weekends and he brought additional work for her to do. Now that the office was organized, she began to have more free time. Addie sensed a hollowness that she had never experienced before. Could it be Adelaide Richards was getting lonesome in this big house?

Ella came into the dining room. "Miss Adelaide, Jess came by and said he has to go to the feed store in town. Can I ride along with him?"

Addie had met Caleb's friend, Jess, only once. Jess was a large man and had that southwestern look with a quiet smile that made one wonder what he was thinking. His coloring and features caused Addie to wonder if there was American Indian in his heritage. He was a decent sort. Still, allowing Ella to go alone with him didn't seem prudent. Addie didn't want to deny the maid the chance to go to town.

Addie sat for a moment. "Ella, I haven't been out of this place in almost two months. If it is all right with Jess, I'll ride along, too."

Ella perked up like a pup spying a rabbit. "Oh, Miss Adelaide. He won't care."

Addie wasn't so sure, but there was no way Jess could refuse. Then an idea popped up, why not ask Lottie, also? Addie hadn't seen her friend since they visited their parents in June.

"Ella, you go tell Jess. I'll run to Miss Lottie's house and he can pick us up there."

Two excited young women went their separate ways with the anticipation of what the day held in store.

As long as they would be back before dinnertime, Lottie was eager to go. "I'll leave a note for Caleb," she said and plunked a straw hat on her head on the way out the door.

Jess was driving the wagon down the lane. He stopped so Addie and Lottie could climb into the bed. If he was miffed at having to take all three young women with him, he didn't show it. Ella was sitting next to him on the buckboard seat.

"Mornin'," he said and touched the brim of his tall cowboy hat, the same kind Caleb wore.

"Good morning," they responded in unison.

Addie helped Lottie up into the wagon and they giggled like schoolgirls before taking a seat in the corner behind the driver.

"It looks like a pretty day, Jess," said Addie. "Thank you for letting us come along."

"Might rain," he answered.

"The sky looks clear to me," enjoined Lottie.

"Might rain," he repeated.

On North Church Street in town, Addie told Jess to stop the wagon so she and Lottie could walk. She didn't want to take a chance on Alex seeing them riding in the farm wagon. She didn't think he would approve.

"You can pick us up here at two-thirty," she told Jess. "Do you want to come with us, Ella?"

"No ma'am."

That was welcome news. It would be just she and Lottie walking the main street of Berryville as they had done so many times.

"Let's go to Coyner's first and then to Mr. White's general store," Addie suggested. "I want a new dress. I've been thinking that if I bought material, you could make one for me."

Lottie sent a knowing look in her friend's direction. "No wonder you brought me along."

"It occurred to me after I thought of asking you. I've got forty dollars. I can buy material for both of us. I don't think either of us have had any new clothes since we came home from the West."

"That's true," agreed Lottie. She contemplated the situation. "Tomatoes are beginning to come in and, once I'm through with all the canning, I'll have time to sew."

They headed east on Main Street.

Addie asked, "Do you like all that work with gardening, putting up vegetables? I hated to see tomatoes. They came in at the hottest time of the summer. And, cucumbers? That vinegar brine we put them in smelled up the whole house. I think my mother pickled anything she could get her hands on."

Lottie laughed. "Your mom was different than mine. My mother is as good at sitting as yours is at being busy."

"You are right about that."

"To answer your question," said Lottie. "Do I like to put food up? The answer is, yes. It's a sense of accomplishment to go into the pantry and see all those filled jars lined up on the shelves and know I was the one who did it." She teased Addie. "You can help me put up the tomatoes."

"I won't have time," came her friend's quick reply.

At Coyner's they went up the two steps that led into the two-story department store. Addie and Lottie turned to the left where the dry goods were kept. There were bolts of material on the shelf behind the wooden counter that had drawers holding pins, buttons, hooks and eyes, thread, and other items that were needed for sewing.

"What do you want the dress for?" asked Lottie.

"No special reason," answered Addie. "I want something that will work for everyday and also for Sunday wear, not that I'll need it."

"Let's find a pattern first," suggested Lottie.

The clerk came to help. They were surprised to see she was one of the girls who had been in their class at school.

Addie gave a quiet cry of surprise. "Nettie? We didn't know you worked here."

With a wide smile of recognition, Nettie exclaimed, "Adelaide and Lottie Bell! I didn't know you were back."

They kept their voices low as they didn't want to disturb Mr. Coyner, whose low-walled office was on a landing area off the steps leading to the upper floor. From where he sat he could see the main floor of the store.

Unexpectedly, Lottie was the one to answer, "We came back a little over a year ago. Addie has been away to school. I'm married and living here on a big farm." Lottie figured that was enough information. "We came to buy material for dresses. First we need patterns."

Nettie had not been a favorite of Lottie's when they were in school; she was the gossipy type. Becoming the knowledgeable sales clerk, Nettie pulled out a drawer that contained Butterick and McCall's patterns. "You can look through these. Styles are changing because of the war. We don't have such a good choice of materials as we had last year."

Lottie became busy finding patterns. If she had to make the dresses, she wanted to be sure they weren't complicated.

Nettie turned to Addie. "You were wise to go on your adventure," she said. "At my mother's urging, George and I got married the summer we graduated. I would like to have had more free time. I am surprised that Lottie Bell is married. What are you doing now? I heard you became a secretary instead of a teacher."

"Yes," Addie answered. "Lottie met her husband while we were in Colorado."

Nettie raised an eyebrow. "I expected you to marry before her."

"I am not so inclined," Addie replied.

"Everyone was disappointed that you didn't go to the teacher's school in Harrisonburg."

Addie offered a sly smile. "I chose to be thoroughly trained as a secretary and bookkeeper."

"Ah, yes. I heard you would be returning to work on that big farm. It was the talk of the town when Mr. Lockwood bought that place." So, it was no surprise to Nettie where Addie was employed. Did she also fake not knowing Lottie was married and living on the farm?

"Why would buying that place be a topic of conversation?" asked a puzzled Addie.

"Mrs. Talley said he didn't come by it honestly."

Addie wanted an explanation. "I don't understand."

Nettie shrugged her shoulder. "It was said that the owner didn't want to sell. Next thing everyone knew, his lawyer owned it. The question was if Mr. Lockwood came by it honestly. At least, that's what Mrs. Talley said."

Before Addie could get any more information, Lottie turned to her with two patterns in hand. "Look at these. What do you think? I want this plain one that I can pull on over my head."

Addie looked at the patterns. "That looks easy and good for doing housework. What is this one you picked out for me? It isn't a dress."

"It says for work or play. I can make a bloused waist in a light material for warmer days. Then a bit heavier material for the skirt and jacket. Fall is around the corner."

Addie viewed the pattern with a closer eye. It would be versatile, and, if she chose a plain material for the skirt, she could wear different colored waists with it. "Can you sew this, Lottie?"

The appointed seamstress nodded. "The jacket may take some doing, but it is not as complicated as it looks. I like the buttons opening down the side of the skirt."

Addie picked out a forest-green colored cotton gabardine for the skirt and jacket and a beige cotton batiste for the waist. She could wear the beige color with her copper and navy skirts.

Lottie's material was cotton broadcloth, dainty flowers on a sea-blue background.

By the time Nettie added up the buttons, thread, lining, and other incidentals, Addie's bill came to twenty-three dollars and twelve cents. She handed one twenty and one five-dollar bill to Nettie, who put the bill of sale and the money into a small container that was attached to a cable leading up to Mr. Coyner's office. He made the change, placed it into the small cylinder and whizzed it back to Nettie on the return cable.

Nettie smiled as she handed the change to Addie. "Mr. Coyner says this method keeps everyone honest," she explained. Quietly she added, "And, I don't have to worry if he makes a mistake."

The young women chuckled.

Addie and Lottie were on their way. "It was nice to see you, Nettie."

The former classmate smiled. "I hope you will be coming back soon."

The two happy women left with their cherished possessions.

"She's going to take Mrs. Talley's place in the nosiness category," remarked Lottie.

"I wonder what people said when we took off for Colorado?" asked an inquisitive Addie.

"Who cares," said Lottie. "I'm getting hungry."

They walked to Mr. White's general store where Addie couldn't resist the paperback books. She bought one about the Lewis and Clark expedition and one about the Civil War. Two white porcelain teacups decorated with small yellow roses caught her eye. They would be a perfect gift for her mother.

Mr. White said that Mrs. Talley had told him about Addie deciding to become a secretary after that "foolhardy trip to Colorado".

"Those were her words, Adelaide. I think you two girls were courageous to strike out on your own."

"Thank you, Mr. White. It was a learning experience for both of us, wasn't it Lottie?"

Lottie was busy looking at the candies. She nodded her agreement.

Addie picked up a few more personal items and paid eleven dollars and fifteen cents.

They thanked Mr. White and left the store.

Addie glanced at her pin which held a watch. It had been a graduation gift from Clayton Lockwood. "We have time for lunch," she said to Lottie. "I've got enough money left to buy a couple of sandwiches. Let's eat at the hotel."

"I thought you wanted to go to Irene Butler's dress shop."

Addie shook her head. "I changed my mind. Her clothing will just make me want to buy what I can't afford. We'll have enough time to have lunch and meet Jess at two-thirty."

After they finished eating, the young women walked by the opera house on Church Street and found Jess and Ella waiting in the appointed spot farther up near Grace Episcopal Church. The sky was beginning to cloud up.

"I think Jess was right. It looks like it might rain," surmised Lottie.

Addie raised her head. "It looks like clouds rolling in. Maybe we'll reach home ahead of the rain. We can put our packages under that canvas in the wagon if we have to."

"I don't want that hard candy I bought to get wet. It'll turn into one big gob."

"I don't think we have anything to worry about," assured Adelaide.

Lottie sent a wry smile in her direction. "You've been wrong before."

When they reached Lockwood under an angry sky, Jess ran the wagon into the barn because he didn't want the feed to get wet. The three young women hopped down from the wagon

"Lottie, come with us," said Addie. "Those are mean clouds. You won't make it home in time."

One look at the dark sky and Lottie knew Addie was right. She hustled along with them to the big house. They had no sooner closed the back door when a thunderous deluge of wind-driven rain pelted the house. Sounds like the roar of a train and the cracking of tree branches caused the three young women to gather together like frightened sheep. There was a boom of thunder that shook the house and rattled the windows.

"The stairs!" cried Addie. "Let's get under the stairs!"

All three crowded into the big closet. They stood among brooms, mops, dust cloths, and outdoor jackets reeking of old sweat as they waited silently until the clashing sounds rolled into the distance.

Addie carefully opened the closet door. The rain had lessened and the sun was coming back out. Three wide-eyed young women emerged from their sanctuary and took deep breaths.

"Miss Adelaide," said Ella, in a nervous voice. "I ain't never seen nor heard a storm like that."

"It scared the bejeepers out of me," admitted Lottie.

Addie breathed a heavy sigh of relief. "Ella, I believe we can all use a cup of tea."

"Right you are, Miss Adelaide. I'll put the kettle on the fire."

Lottie had tossed the bag from Coyner's onto a chair before they headed for the closet. "I don't think anything fell out of the bag, but I'd better make sure."

She placed the bag on the kitchen table and began to check the contents.

Addie picked up the pattern for her outfit and gave a light brush of her hand over the forest green gabardine. "Lottie, this is going to be perfect. I can hardly wait."

"You'll have to wait until I'm through canning those tomatoes," reminded Lottie. "Sure you don't want to help?"

"I'm not in that much of a hurry," replied her friend. "Let's clear this stuff away and have our tea."

CHAPTER 11

Alex arrived at the farm on Saturday morning. He questioned if there had been any costly damage to the place from the ferocious storm a couple of days ago because telephone lines were down and he hadn't been able to reach the house.

Addie was in the office. "You'll have to ask Caleb. I know there were a few trees down," she told him. Seeing Alex brought to mind what Nettie had said when they were in town, and Addie wanted to ask him how he had acquired Lockwood. At one time he had said that it was an unexpected opportunity. The possibility there had been some underhanded dealing did not appeal to her.

Alex informed, "I have some men coming this afternoon to discuss selling goods to the government. I would like to have a good dinner for them. James Anderson will be here, also."

Addie looked up under hooded eyelids. "Do you expect me to handle the details?"

"Certainly."

The announcement did not set well. "It would have been nice to have some warning. You have a telephone."

He countered, "The lines were down."

"Have you told Ella?"

Half an apologetic smile appeared. "No, I thought you could do that."

Addie sat straight up in her chair and looked at him. "You know the news is going to throw her into a tizzy. How many guests do you expect?"

"Four plus James."

"No wives or unencumbered females?"

Alex laughed aloud. "Why, Miss Richards. How you do go on." He added, "None that I know of."

"Good," she replied. "That makes it easier. Men won't care about the incidentals if they are fed a good meal."

He came around the desk where he took both her hands in his. "Then I shall leave it all up to you." He was off to find his foreman.

Addie sat speechless. His touch was like a shock of electricity surging through her body. She felt the heat in her face and patted her cheeks to cool them down before she went in search of Ella.

When the news was given to the young maid, she flew into a dither as Addie expected she would.

Ella's hands flew up in the air. "Oh, Miss Adelaide. I ain't got time to fix a big dinner and I ain't got a cake or pie or anythin' else ready. Oh, dear Lord, what am I gonna do, I didn't 'spect nothin' like this, I…"

"Hold on, Ella. Take a deep breath and we'll figure out what to do." Addie put her thoughts to work. "You can make chicken and dumplings, potatoes, and we'll think of something else."

"I ain't got a chicken."

"There are plenty out in the chicken yard. I'll help you get one."

Ella was wide-eyed. "Do you know how to kill a chicken?"

"I don't like to but I can if I have to," said a confident Addie.

"Can't we get one of the men to do it?"

"There isn't time. Put the ham boiler over and fill it with water. We need it boiling. The water can be heating while we run down the chicken."

While Ella put the water over, Addie went to the barn and found a hatchet. It would be nice if it had a sharper edge, but it would handle the job.

The two apprehensive women entered the chicken yard and the chickens flew everywhere. "Let's get that big red one over near the fence," said Addie.

Ella threw a handful of corn and the chicken started pecking at it. Addie held a pillowcase and threw it over the bird. Both of the women pounced and captured the unsuspecting chicken, but it was a hassle trying to hold on. Addie managed to grab its legs after a struggle. She carried it to a stump that had plenty of scars from decapitated chickens.

"Here, Ella. You've got to grab around its middle and hold onto its feet. I can't do anything with it flopping its wings like that."

"What are you going to do?" asked a nervous Ella.

"I'm going to stretch its neck and cut off its head."

"I ain't gonna' watch."

64

Addie was getting exasperated. "Then turn your head, but hold onto the chicken or we won't have anything for dinner."

Ella was squeezing the hen and holding the legs with all her might.

Addie positioned herself close to the stump pulled the head of the chicken toward her, and gave one solid whack with the hatchet. "Let it go," she hollered to Ella, who had blood spattered on her apron.

The shaking girl let go and off flew the headless chicken. "That hen's still alive," Ella shouted.

Addie wiped her sweaty forehead with the back of her hand. "No, that's the nerves dying. Once it stops flopping around, we'll douse it in the boiling water and pick the feathers."

"Are you gonna' gut it?" asked Ella.

Addie rested her hand on her hip. "I suppose I'll have to, if you don't know how."

If Ella knew how, she wasn't going to let on to Addie. The smell of warm gutted chicken was enough to turn anyone's stomach.

"I'll get the oven and stuffin' ready." The maid was returning to lucidity. "I believe I can bake a cherry cobbler in the oven along with the chicken."

"We can get tomatoes and corn from the garden," advised Addie. "That should be a dinner to satisfy any man."

"Oh, Miss Adelaide, I don't know what I woulda' done if you weren't here."

Addie didn't know either. "Let's pluck this chicken. Once it's ready to go in the oven, you can concentrate on food and I'll prepare the table."

The big red sorry-looking bird lay on its side. Addie picked up the lifeless chicken, still dripping spots of blood, and the two resourceful young women headed to the house for the next step in the process.

Three hours later, the six men arrived for dinner. They had washed their hands out by the well.

Addie had the dining table set with a tan damask tablecloth and napkins to match. Silver utensils, water glasses, brown pottery mugs and plates, made the room feel comfortable for the men. As a centerpiece, she tied brown rick-rack around a short spray of dried wheat. On a side table sat two bottles of wine and wine glasses. Alex could pour, if the men were so inclined. Addie took one more glance around the room before she went to the kitchen to help the maid.

Ella was slicing the baked chicken. "I got everythin' else warmin' on the top of the stove."

"Good," replied Adelaide. "The men are coming in the front door."

"Lordy, I hope I done everythin' right. I'm jumpy as a cat."

Addie put her hand on Ella's shoulder. "Look at me."

Ella stopped slicing and met Addie's eyes.

"You have done a wonderful job of pulling this together. Those men in there don't care how the food is served, they just want to fill their bellies. I'll put the rest of the food in the serving dishes and get a platter for the chicken."

Addie opened the cupboard door and pulled out bowls. "One thing, Ella."

"What's that?"

"I suggest you change your apron before you take the food in. It's still got splotches of blood from our unfortunate hen."

Alex came into the kitchen. "Smells great in here. The men are having a glass of wine, and, Ella, you can bring the food in. Adelaide, I'd like to have you record this meeting."

The all-business Alex had returned.

Addie's look was unpleasant, but he didn't seem to notice. "Is that during dinner or after? I would like to change into something more presentable."

"After dessert will be soon enough."

Ella had put on a clean apron. She loaded up a serving cart and took it to the dining room where she placed the dishes on a buffet. The men could serve themselves.

Addie hurried into her room where she changed into her white waist and copper skirt. She brushed her hair, tinted her cheeks with rouge and powdered her nose. She was both jittery and annoyed. Did Alex realize the situation he had put both her and Ella in? Perhaps he didn't, but Adelaide would set him straight so it wouldn't happen again.

She picked up her pencil and stenographic notebook. One look in the mirror told her she looked poised and efficient.

When she arrived in the dining room, all six men stood.

"Gentlemen, this is my secretary, Miss Richards. I have asked her to record our meeting."

The men gave appreciative smiles and nodded in her direction.

James Anderson addressed her. "It's nice to see you again, Miss Richards."

He was as breathtaking as the first time she had seen him, but this time she was prepared. She offered a demure smile before taking her seat in the corner of the room.

The men explained that, with the war going on, the government was buying all kinds of merchandise. "They need grain, meat, hides, wool, about everything they can get their hands on," said one of the men.

James Anderson made clear his knowledge of horses, especially horses that could be trained for combat and those needed for strenuous work. He knew all the farms in the area and could procure not only horses but also mules.

By the time the men were ready to leave, much had been settled. As they were getting ready to depart, James Anderson came to where Addie sat. "It is a big help to all of us for you to take these notes of our meeting. If you ever get tired of working for Alex, I could use your talents at my place."

It was not difficult to see why James Anderson was still a favorite among young ladies. He had a charismatic charm.

"Thank you. I'm quite happy here at Lockwood."

He held his plaid driving cap in his hand. With a half-smile and nod of his head, he said, "Goodbye, Miss Richards."

James placed the cap on his head as he joined the others who were leaving. Dusk was setting in. The four men climbed into a Model T Ford while James settled into a sporty-looking, two seat auto.

Addie closed her notebook and rose from the chair. She went to the kitchen where the maid was cleaning up. "Ella, the men have gone. I'll help you clear off the dining table."

Ella had a couple of hours of work ahead of her and the one light bulb suspended from a long cord from the ceiling wasn't going to be much help. "Why don't you leave some of that until morning?" suggested Addie.

"Do you think Mr. Alex will mind? I am tired."

"So am I," replied Addie. "Mr. Lockwood isn't going to care as long as it doesn't look like a big mess if he happens to wander into the kitchen."

"Then I'm goin' to leave them heavy things soakin'. Good night, Miss Adelaide."

"Good night, Ella."

Addie noticed the lamp in the office was on and she saw Alex looking through a ledger. She entered the room. "Can I help you find something?" she asked.

He looked up. The smile in his warm brown eyes was comforting. "Come in and sit."

She sat in the armchair at the side of the desk. He leaned back in his chair twirling a pencil between his fingers. "Addie, I believe this place is going to pay for itself. The war may end up to be a terrible thing for some, but for me it's going to be profitable. Everything we have on the farm is something the government is going to need."

Addie wasn't sure how to voice her concern but she had to know. "Lottie and I went into town the other day. A clerk in Mr. Coyner's store said there were questions about how you had attained this property."

He stopped twirling the pencil. "Do you think I was underhanded?"

She shook her head. "No. It bothered me to hear that kind of talk."

"I'm sure it did." He sat forward in his chair. "I have always, and will continue to be, honest in my dealings, Adelaide. I was the lawyer for the gentleman who owned this estate. His health was failing and he did not want to wait for a buyer." Alex paused. "Addie, he asked me to take it off his hands so he could move close to relatives near Roanoke. I wasn't sure I could afford to take the chance, but we were able to work out a deal that was fair to both him and me."

His explanation caused relief. "I am not sorry I asked. I was quite sure that you attained it without shady dealings."

"But not quite sure enough," he responded. "I would prefer that you would have more faith in me than to have doubts."

Addie was quick to say, "Alex, I regret that I felt the need to ask."

"So am I," he answered.

"If my words were hurtful, I am sorry. Will you forgive me?"

He sat for a moment. "I realize how the accusation must have sounded to you. For both of us, it was good that you brought it into the open. You did nothing wrong so there is no need for forgiveness. Friends again?"

She offered a relieved smile. "Friends again," she affirmed. "It has been a tiring day. If you don't need me for anything, I'm going off to bed."

"It has been an exhausting day for me, too," he said. "Addie, I'm glad you're here."

She got up from the chair. "Good night, Alex."

He raised a questioning eyebrow. "I shall see you for breakfast in the morning?"

"Bright eyed and bushy tailed," she answered.

CHAPTER 12

A week later, Addie was looking out the office window when she saw a rider on horseback coming up the drive. Recognition caused her pulse to quicken. She ran out the front door and down the steps. "Clay!" she hollered as she waved at him.

He rode to where she stood and bounded from the saddle. "Addie!" In a warm hug, his strong arms raised her up until her feet left the ground before he released her.

"Why haven't you come sooner? You must have known I was here."

He didn't answer immediately as he eyed her from head to toe. "It took me a long time to get over your letter of rejection. You are a sight for sore eyes."

His words caused her to be ill at ease. "It was not a rejection letter. It was an answer to the one you sent tagging me as your girl. I thought it best to tell you where I stood. I was sure you were lonely and down in the dumps at the university. Come sit on the porch. Do you want a glass of water?"

"It was a hot and dusty ride. I can use one."

Clay settled his brawn in a rocker. He took off his riding hat and wiped his face with a handkerchief. His dark hair glistened with sweat and his ruddy face glowed from the ride in the heat of the day.

Addie opened the front door and called, "Ella, please bring two glasses and a pitcher of water out to the porch." She took a seat in the rocker next to Clay. "Tell me about your studies and what decisions you have made."

"That's the reason I came…"

Ella arrived with a tray holding the glasses and pitcher of cold water.

"Ella, this is Mr. Clay. He's a brother to Mr. Alex."

Clay offered an appreciative smile. "My brother employs pretty girls," he remarked.

The flustered maid's face turned beet red.

"Thank you, Ella," said Addie. "That's all we need."

The embarrassed young girl scuttled back into the house, stealing a side glance at Mr. Clay Lockwood.

"That wasn't nice to tease her," corrected Adelaide.

He grinned. "I was being truthful. She is a very pretty girl."

"Yes, she is. I don't think she has had much exposure to the world. In fact, I don't believe she can read and write."

He laughed aloud. "I'm sure Alex didn't hire her for those qualities."

Addie sat up straight in the rocker. "Clayton Lockwood what has gotten into you?"

"All that university training," he answered. "I'm leaving, Addie."

"You just got here. You can't go yet."

He assumed a somber tone. "No. I mean I am leaving home. I'm going into the military."

She was struck dumb and it took her a moment to recover. "You're serious about this, aren't you?"

He nodded. "Some of the boys around here are joining up. You know I haven't been satisfied with college life. I'm going into the cavalry. They train men and horses at Fort Sill in Oklahoma. I leave Saturday morning."

"Oklahoma? That's where Lottie's husband is from. You should meet Caleb."

The air of conversation was lighter. "How is Lottie? Gosh, I haven't seen you girls in two years."

Addie smiled. "She loves being married and all that domestic stuff that goes with it. She and Caleb live in the house over there," she said and pointed to the small brick house in the distance. "Want to go see her?"

"I don't have time. Too many loose ends to tie up before I go."

Setting his empty water glass on a small wicker table, he stood and walked around the porch taking in the view, pausing to take in the panorama of the Blue Ridge Mountains in the distance. "Alex has got quite a place here," he remarked. "Maybe one day I'll have the same thing."

"His plans are to give up his law practice if the farm can sustain itself. With the war going on, it looks promising for the farms. There were men out here last week who procure for the government."

"Alex always seems to come out the winner."

Addie looked over at the young man who had been her childhood playmate. "Don't forget that Alex is sixteen years older than you. Certainly you wouldn't regret him making a go of it."

After a thoughtful moment, he said, "Maybe there's a tad of jealously in me." He came to where she sat pulling her to standing. "I couldn't leave without seeing you. Is everything working out for you here?"

"So far," she answered. "Alex loaned the money for my schooling, and I am paying him back. My debt will be paid in March. Who knows? I may be exploring other opportunities if there are no changes around here."

Clay's face was close to hers. "What might those changes be?"

She didn't answer his question. "Clay, I think you are doing the right thing. You can finish up your year at the university when you leave the service, if you care to."

Her words were lost on him. "I'm going to kiss you, Adelaide Richards. I'll carry the memory just like I did that stolen kiss when you showed me your hat. We sat on that fallen log on a beautiful day in June. Do you remember?"

She had to smile as she recalled the scene. "I do. This is one kiss that I will gladly give. I hate to see you go."

His warm full lips covered hers and he held her close.

"Keep yourself safe," she whispered.

He released her and took her hand. "I promise. I'm going to write to you, Addie."

She felt tears welling up within. "I am so pleased you came. I would have been so disappointed if you had gone off without telling me. We did have fun growing up on your parents' farm, didn't we." It was a statement instead of a question to which he nodded his approval.

"You'll write to me?" Clay asked.

"As often as I can," she replied.

Clay kissed the fingers of the hand he held, turned, and went down the steps. He eased his hefty body up into the saddle. With a wave of one hand, he used the other to guide the horse down the drive.

Addie watched as he rode out of sight. She could still feel the warmth of his kiss and the touch of his hand. "You like Clay, You don't love him," Lottie had once said. She was right, but Clay Lockwood had stirred feelings that she had not experienced before.

Addie took the tray with glasses and water pitcher into the house. She addressed Ella, who was busy in the kitchen. "I'm going to run over to Miss Lottie's house. I'll be back in an hour."

"Mr. Clay don't look anythin' like Mr. Alex," said Ella.

Addie gave a half-smile. "No, they are quite different in many ways."

"Do you want I should make dinner for you?"

"No, it's too hot. There is some ham left in the icebox, I'll make a sandwich later on."

"Is Mr. Alex goin' to bring more men when he comes?" asked a concerned Ella.

"I don't believe we have to worry about that. He is to call if he will be having guests for dinner."

Ella breathed a sigh of relief. "I don't want to see any more chickens' heads chopped off."

Addie wagged her head and went out the back door.

Lottie was canning tomatoes when Addie arrived. Her face was red and she was sweating like a horse. The room was hot and steaming. She had pulled her hair on top of her head and secured it with a rubber band causing the ends to fan out like a peacock, only not as graceful.

"Gads, Lottie, how can you enjoy doing this?" Addie said as she fanned her face with her hand.

"I didn't say I enjoyed the process; I like to see the pretty jars when I'm finished. What brings you here?"

"You will never guess who just came by the house."

"Clay Lockwood."

Addie's jaw dropped. "How did you know?"

Lottie was filling hot jars with hot tomatoes. "I knew it wasn't either of our parents, and we don't know anybody else that would cause you to hustle over here."

Lottie wiped the rim of the jar, placed a rubber seal around it, put on the glass top and secured the wire clamp. "What did Clay want?"

"He's going into the army. He leaves day after tomorrow. Guess where he's going?"

Lottie looked over at her friend. "Is this question and answer day?"

"He's going to Oklahoma to be trained for the cavalry."

The news did not phase Lottie. She stood back admiring the dozen quart jars of bright red tomatoes.

"I'm done," she announced. "Let's sit outdoors. Want some cold tea?"

"Yes. I'll meet you outside."

Addie stepped out of the house onto a covered back porch. The air was still too warm but cooler than inside. Lottie had put layers of cotton batting on the tops of two sturdy crates and covered them with oilcloth. Addie took a seat.

Out came Lottie carrying two glasses of cold tea and handed one to her friend. "Now, tell me about Clay."

Addie told her about their friend, about the government men coming, and about the dinner Alex sprang on her and Ella. They chatted for forty-five minutes before Addie decided she should get back to finish up in the office.

"You look tired, Lottie," she observed. "I hope you're not overdoing. I could have Ella come and help."

"I think it's the heat of the summer. Ella has enough to do taking care of the big house. When is Alex going to hire someone to help her?"

Addie stood to leave. "Those are the kinds of questions I don't ask."

"Throw a hint in his direction."

Addie laughed. "I suppose I could do that."

Lottie Bell remained on the make-do seat.

"Bye, Lottie."

CHAPTER 13

Friday morning the telephone rang shortly after Addie had finished breakfast. She went into the office, took the receiver off the hook and put it to her ear. It was Alex.

"I called to let you know that I will not be coming by tomorrow until late in the afternoon. My parents are having a get-together this evening for Clay. He is going into the military."

"Yes, I know," replied Addie. "Clay came by the other day."

There was silence on the other end for a moment. "What do you think of his plan?"

"I think it is what Clay needs. He's enthused. Perhaps it will help him decide what he wants to do when he returns."

Alex changed the subject, "How are things out on the farm?"

"There still is debris to clean up from the storm. To my knowledge, everything else is going well. Caleb said they will begin haying next week."

Alex contemplated aloud. "I should check with Jane to see if she can watch the office a couple extra days."

"Whatever you think best," Addie responded.

"Do you need anything from town? We will have to feed the men that come to help with the haying."

We, thought Addie. He means me and Ella. "I will check with Ella and call you back. If you don't hear from me, then you can assume that we have enough on hand."

"Good thinking," he answered.

She bit her tongue. "That's what I'm here for. Goodbye, Alex."

"Wait! I have a man from town coming to slaughter and roast one of the pigs. That should take care of meat." He chuckled into the phone. "I don't want you to have to behead any more of the chickens."

"Goodbye, Alex." She hung up the receiver with a healthy plop.

It was up to her to break the news to Ella. The meat was taken care of and that was a help, but Addie knew haying season meant sweat-soaked men with big appetites. Sometimes families accompanied the workers. It was a chance for women to get out of the house and catch up on the local happenings or gossip. And, if wives came, they brought their children and a food dish of some sort. There would be plenty of mouths to feed.

Addie thought it wise to confer with Caleb as to how many would be coming before she passed the word to the flighty maid. Caleb was working near the stables when she reached him.

"Hello, Caleb."

He stopped his task, throwing a pitchfork into a stack of hay. He offered a lop-sided grin. "Hi, Addie. What brings you down here?"

"It isn't the smell. Boy, it stinks around here in the heat of summer. I need to know how many to expect when you start haying next week."

He pushed his tall cowboy back and wiped his forehead with a handkerchief. "There's four of us and I figure five more. They can't get here 'til eight. We might finish in a day."

"Are they bringing wives and family?"

"I 'spect so."

"That's close enough," she said. "I'll check with Lottie on the way back and see if she can help."

His look was concern. "I don't think Lottie's feelin' too good. I don't ask 'cause I can be a worrier. After that scare we had in Colorado, when she almost died, it caused me to pay close attention."

"I was by last week and noticed she looks tired. She has been working hard putting up those tomatoes, and, in this heat, that is bound to tire anyone."

"I guess you're most likely right. We start hayin' Monday."

Addie held her nose. "I wish that breeze would change direction. The odor from the manure bothers my stomach."

He pulled his stained tall hat back square on his head and laughed. "I don't even notice. See you, Addie."

She should check in with Lottie, but her house was a distance away from the stables. Back to the big house Addie walked, rehearsing words in her head and dreading how Ella was going to accept the news.

The slim young girl was hauling a bucket of water out of the well. She saw Addie approach. "Miss Addie, I thought you was in the office."

"I had to find Caleb to ask him a question. They are going to start bringing in the hay on Monday. He has five men coming to help. He says they will bring their families with them."

"That'll be nice to have visitors."

Addie hesitated. "What do you think if I tell you we have to feed them all?"

Ella was stunned and dropped the bucket of water. "That can't be. Miss Addie I don't know anythin' about feedin' a bunch of people." Then she started to shake and cry. "I can't, I can't, I just can't." She blubbered into her apron.

Although Adelaide felt sorry for Ella, the girl needed to learn to handle ups and downs of life. "We got through feeding those government men and we'll get through this. Mr. Alex has taken care of the meat. There's a man coming to roast a pig. We will just have to do the rest."

Ella wiped her red eyes. "I didn't mean to cry. I didn't know I was goin' to have to do stuff like this."

"If it makes you feel any better, I didn't either. Let's go into the house and see what is on

83

hand. Mr. Alex can bring whatever we need from the store, but I have to know what that would be."

Ella refilled the bucket with water and they went into the house together.

Addie went to the office and returned to the kitchen with a pencil and paper. She took a paring knife from the drawer and sharpened the point of the pencil. "I'm going to write down what foods we have and we can decide from there. Come sit at the table with me and tell me what foods we have."

The reluctant maid took a seat. "I know there's lots of potatoes and tomatoes, and corn."

"That's a good start. How about dried beans?"

Ella went to the cupboard and pulled out a large pot. "I ain't had time to sort them," she apologized.

"I can help with that." Addie tapped her lip with the end of the pencil as she thought. "If the women bring a dish, it will be some kind of dessert, I'm sure."

"How do you know that?" asked Ella.

"I had to help when I was growing up. I remember that women always brought something sweet. They liked to show off cakes, and cookies, that kind of thing. I'll check with Lottie. If she can make a couple of apple pies, then we should have enough. You'll have to bake bread, which means flour, yeast, sugar, butter…"

"I know there's plenty of that stuff," Ella interrupted.

Addie finished the list and reviewed it. "Tea, coffee?"

"Yes, ma'am. And, there's plenty of ice in the ice house."

The ice house had been a brainstorm for Alex. He had read how dairy farmers kept milk and products fresh in a concrete building, so he had a smaller one constructed on the farm. It served more than one purpose of keeping ice longer; on sweltering days a person could duck inside and get cooled off for a moment of relief, and it held extra milk, butter, cream and cottage cheese. The floor, ceiling and sides were all concrete with air space at the top and sloped for drainage at the floor. Addie had learned about Eskimos and igloos built of ice and wondered if this concrete hut was similar. She had no desire to live as an Eskimo.

Addie went through the list item by item. "We will have to prepare for thirty people. That means five times as much food as we prepared when we had to get dinner for six."

"How do you know that?" asked an astonished Ella.

Addie raised an eyebrow. "Ella, how much schooling have you had?"

She looked down at her toes. "I went through the second grade."

"So you know a little about reading and arithmetic."

"Not much," she answered.

"Would you like to learn more?"

Her eyes brightened. "Yes, ma'am."

Addie brightened also. "Once we get this haying business over, we can spend an hour of each day learning." If she could get Ella up to a fifth grade level in both subjects, she felt the young girl would be able to survive on her own. For the moment, haying was two days away and there were preparations to make.

"We will need ten loaves of bread. I'll start sorting the beans."

"Ten loaves of bread! That's goin' to take a powerful lot of flour," surmised Ella.

"Yes, with the potatoes, corn, tomatoes, and beans that should be enough to stick to their ribs."

Ella laughed aloud. "Miss Addie, I ain't never heard that before."

Addie smiled, "It sounds better than 'to fill up their gullets'."

"That one I have heard," chuckled Ella. "I guess we'd best get started."

CHAPTER 14

By eight o'clock Monday morning, Addie and Ella had been busy for three hours. Lottie arrived with two big apple pies and tiredness still in her eyes. The hired men had set up a table made of wood planks placed across wood sawhorses. Addie had a table cloth of cotton muslin and Lottie brought another. They didn't match but together they were enough to cover the make-shift table top and prevent the guests from getting splinters.

The workers arrived. Neither Addie nor Lottie knew the five wives who accompanied their husbands, although last names sounded familiar, but the wives knew each other. After initial introductions, the visiting women began talking about their children, cooking, sewing, and what they had heard about this one and that one, or whatever news was going around in the farm circles. Lottie sat with them and listened to their palaver. Addie found the conversation mundane. Besides, someone had to keep an eye on the children. The mothers were oblivious to where their offspring were or what they were into.

Shortly after noon, the men came in for lunch. They were hot, sweat-soaked and hungry just as Addie expected. Most had faces red or leathery from days in the sun and a light ring around their foreheads where their hats sat. They ranged in height from tall to short and body builds from stocky to slim but all had taut muscles that spoke of day after day of hard work.

The women pitched in to help with serving food. The men asked Alex about selling to the government. As though he was an authority on the subject, they listened in polite silence as he expounded his knowledge of what he had learned.

Addie was observant. She watched Ella keep a steady pace, intent on making sure there was enough food on the table. The young girl did not take notice of the admiring glances of the men. The women cast a wary eye at Ella, and judiciously scrutinized Jess. This made Addie smile inwardly. As Clay had observed, Alexander Lockwood, noted lawyer in the county, employed pretty young girls at his farm. He also employed a handsome hired man. What tales will be spawned from this day of haying at Lockwood farm?

By five o'clock in the afternoon, it was time for the helpers to pack up and go home. What hay was left in the field could be gathered by the hired men.

Lottie stayed to help clean up. "I'm glad that's over," she said as she sat in one of the kitchen chairs.

Addie plopped down in a chair beside her. "You seemed to fit right in with the farm wives." She brushed her hair off her forehead. "When Alex asked me to take care of the affairs on this place, I didn't picture myself cooking and serving food. I had enough of that growing up."

She looked over at the young maid, who appeared tired enough to drop. "Ella, come and sit for a couple of minutes. You've been on your feet since five o'clock this morning," offered Addie.

"That's true all right," agreed Ella. "But, if I sit I might not be able to get back up."

Lottie took off her shoes and wiggled her toes. "I know what you mean. I could stretch out on this hard wood floor and fall fast asleep."

Addie pooh-poohed those words. "You're just saying that. I remember how you used to complain about the mattress in the boarding house."

Lottie rubbed one tired foot at a time. "That was a hard mattress. You got the good one that the mice had ruffled up some nice stuffing."

Addie laughed. "I offered it to you and you turned up your nose."

"I wasn't sure all the mice were out of it."

Addie rose from the chair. She bent forward and back and sideways stretching to relieve the stiffness she felt. "Yet it was fine for me to use it."

Lottie looked up with a half-smile. "Animals like you better than they do me."

"Lottie Bell Foster!" exclaimed Addie.

"Dunn," Lottie corrected. "I'm married to Caleb Dunn and in a few months there will be a little Dunn."

Addie stretched her arms above her head before Lottie's words hit her. She stopped, lowered her arms and slowly looked over at her friend. "Are you sure?"

"I am. My tiredness isn't from working too hard or the heat of summer. I figure March should see a baby on this farm."

Addie hurried to where Lottie sat and put her arms around her. "I am so happy for you. This is what you have wanted."

Ella turned from the stove with a big smile on her face.

Lottie cautioned, "You two have to keep it a secret because I haven't told Caleb. I am feeling better. I've had a few months of morning sickness but I think that has passed. I'm not telling Caleb for another month. I understand that it is usually within the first three months when things can go wrong."

"Don't have those kinds of thoughts." Addie tapped Lottie's shoulder before returning to the chair she had vacated. "The first baby on Lockwood farm. I can hardly wait." Then she remembered having to help birth her little sister and sat up straight. "I don't want to be around to help deliver it!"

Lottie cast a wry grin. "Gosh darn, Addie. I was going to call you as soon as I got the first pain."

Lottie put on her shoes and was tying the laces. "It was a nice day all in all. I wish we could get into town more or go to the cinema or something."

"I don't see why we can't," said Addie. "Alex is in town every day. I'll ask him to check on what's coming to the opera house. Caleb needs some time away from here. We'll take Ella and Jess also. That way there will be two men and three women and Caleb won't refuse if Jess is going."

"You're full of ideas," said Lottie.

It was close to six o'clock. "I will ask Alex when he comes in. We can plan to go either next Friday or Saturday evening." Addie hadn't been this excited since she had made the decision to go out West.

The thought of the picture show was pleasing to Lottie. "I've cut out my dress material from the pattern, and I've got your waist pinned and ready to cut. The tomatoes are out of the way, so I think I will have enough time to sew the material this week. We could have new clothes to wear."

The possibility was getting rosier by the moment. "Oh, Lottie! New clothes and going to the cinema? I can't wait!"

They had forgotten Ella who was standing at the stove watching and listening.

"Ella, I'm sorry. I almost forgot you were over there. How about it? Would you like to go to the moving picture show?" asked Addie.

"I ain't for sure. How much does it cost?"

"I'll pay for your ticket," said a generous Adelaide. "We're going to ask Jess if he wants to go, too. We'll have a grand time."

Ella grinned from ear to ear. "I ain't never been to a picture show."

"Then it's time you did," said Lottie as she rose from the chair. "I put back some food for Caleb's dinner. He'll be hungry and I helped with enough food for one day."

"Do you want me to walk you home?" asked Addie.

91

Lottie grimaced at her friend. "I'm expecting, not helpless. Ask me again in about six months. Bye, Ella."

"Bye, Miss Lottie. Thanks for helpin' and for your pies."

"Oops, I forgot the pie tins. Addie you can bring them over on Tuesday. I'll need to fit that waist on you."

Addie had moved to the sink. "I will. Is two o'clock good?"

"Make it one," replied Lottie. "Two o'clock is my nap time." Out the door she went.

"You and Miss Lottie are right good friends, aren't you Miss Addie?" asked Ella.

A reminiscent smile creased Addie's face. "We are that," she replied.

Alex came into the house a bit later by the back door. Ella was in the kitchen cleaning soiled dishes when he arrived. "Do you want I should make dinner?" she asked.

"No, I'll pull something out of the icebox. Where's Miss Addie?"

"I ain't for sure."

Alex put pulled pork between two slices of bread before he went in search of his secretary. He heard the clack-clack of the Royal typewriter and knew she was working in the office.

Standing in the doorway, he watched as she efficiently finished a letter and rolled it up into her hands. She looked up and smiled at him. "You look like your hired men, red-faced with a ring around your forehead."

He entered the room and sat in the armchair next to the desk and ran a hand through his thick, disheveled hair. He smiled back at her. "I feel like one." He watched as some chaff fell onto his shirt where he brushed it off. "All I did was supervise and I feel like I was run over by a train. Every joint is stiff. It makes me appreciate my workers who do this kind of thing day in and day out." He took a bite of the sandwich he had carried in.

The opening was perfect. "Lottie and I want to go to the cinema in Berryville with Caleb, Jess and Ella. All three of them need some time from the farm. We want you to check and see what is playing next week."

He placed a booted foot across his knee. "A night out for everyone? I'll check it out and let you know."

She blurted out, "I haven't been to an opera house since we saw the Sousa band at the Tabor Opera House in Leadville."

He shook his head. "Seeing as the cinema is in the back of the opera house in Berryville, I don't think it will compare." A serious note was heard in his voice. "We did have a good time, didn't we?"

She leaned back in her chair with a dreamy look. "It was grand, Alex. I shall never forget that evening."

"Nor will I," he admitted. "You looked lovely. It was refreshing to walk in the crisp night air and to sit with you as though we were the only two people in the world. No one knew us and no one else mattered."

"It was like that at Caleb's mine shack, too. You, me, Caleb and Lottie. Why can't you be as carefree as you were then?" Addie hadn't meant to put her thoughts into words, but she had done it.

He finished the sandwich and moved to a more comfortable position in the armchair. "It's different here, Addie. In case you haven't noticed, I am a prominent lawyer, and I need to guard my reputation."

She handed him a cloth napkin she kept at the desk. "People talk anyway. Clay made a remark about the pretty young maid. I saw the men who came today giving Ella the once over. Don't you think they conjure up their own ideas?"

These words irritated Alex. "Let them think what they want. As long as I keep my nose clean, it is only speculation. As far as Clay is concerned, he takes notice of attractive women. He needs to grow up!"

The unexpected retort caused her to hold a sarcastic reply. When she spoke her voice was timid, "You will check to see what is playing at the picture show?"

Alex sat for a moment and looked at his hands. "If I'm going to run this farm one day, I had better toughen up these hands." He stood, took both her hands and pulled her to her feet. "Just for you, I will check. Addie, you did an exemplary job pulling everything together. You're my number one gal as Caleb would say."

She looked into his kind, brown eyes as a wan smile crossed her lips. If only I were, thought she.

CHAPTER 15

Lottie was waiting when Addie arrived for her fitting on Tuesday. The Singer sewing machine Leopold Goldman had shipped from Leadville was on the kitchen table ready to be put into use.

Addie smiled when she saw it. "I can't believe he sent you that sewing machine, stingy as he is."

"He has a kind heart, although he doesn't want anyone to know it. Do you want a cup of tea?"

"No thanks, I've got to be back at the house at three. Alex has bought a bull and more cattle that are being delivered today. I have to document all of that information. Caleb makes sure that we receive what was expected and I have to be sure it is properly filed so each head can be traced."

Lottie had cut out the material for the waist she was sewing for Addie. The pieces had been pinned together and lay on the table.

"Do you like doing that kind of work?" Lottie asked.

Addie shrugged. "There are times when I wish I was someplace else. Remember when I thought Alex had romantic thoughts for me? I had visions that working right next to him would be ideal. I was wrong. We rarely work side by side."

Addie unbuttoned the waist she was wearing. "Nobody can see, can they?"

"Who's around to see? They're all out working."

Lottie put the pinned material on Addie and began making adjustments. She removed two straight pins, held them between her teeth, tightened a side seam and repined it. "This is going to be pretty. What skirt are you going to wear with this?"

"The navy blue one. Have you finished your dress?"

"All but the hem. I want you to pin it for me when I'm done."

"That's a fair exchange," said Addie. "I am so excited about having an evening away I've been floating on air."

Lottie chuckled. "I'd like to see that. If I look up at the big house and see a levitated figure, I'll know it's you and not have a heart attack."

Addie offered a sideward glance and wrinkled her forehead. "Alex called and said "The Little American" is the picture this week. Mary Pickford is the star; it's directed by Cecil B. DeMille. They are both big names in Hollywood. He said it's a movie about the war."

Lottie mulled over the information. "That should keep Caleb and Jess interested. I'd rather see something with Charlie Chaplin, but as long as we can get away from here for an evening, I don't care what's playing."

Lottie finished fitting the waist and Addie began redressing in the one she had worn. "We should make it a point to get away. You're stuck here all day and I'm stuck up there. I've been wanting to visit my Aunt Lilly down in Boyce. Maybe we could take our mothers along. Make a full day of it."

Lottie put on the dress she had made for herself. "What do you think Addie?"

"Didn't that turn out nice! You have a good eye for picking material and patterns. Stand up on the chair and I'll pin the hem. This dress is going to serve you perfectly. You can hide your secret from Caleb for a couple more months if you want to."

Lottie laughed. "Why do you think I picked out this style? Once you take care of the hem then you can hurry on back before the stock is delivered."

"That's fine with me," replied Addie as she began turning up and pinning the material for Lottie's dress.

"Does Caleb want to go Friday or Saturday?"

"Saturday." Lottie turned on the chair so Adelaide could pin the other side.

Addie was forthright. "We should leave before six o'clock because the show starts at seven. I want a good seat."

"Not that there are a lot to choose from," answered Lottie.

The hem was pinned and Addie helped her friend down from the kitchen chair. "Why don't you bring my waist up to the house on Friday around noontime and Ella can make lunch for us?"

"I wish Ella had something new to wear," mused Lottie. "She's going to feel left out."

"Have you got any more of that curtain material? That would make a pretty kerchief."

Lottie went to the chest where she kept scraps of material. "Here's the lace that's left over. It even has a ruffled edge."

Addie held it up. The lace was a rose and ivy pattern throughout. "I can sew a couple of snaps on the front where it comes together and she can wear it around her neck. The lace is so open I don't think I could go too wrong. Are you sure you don't need this?"

"Take it. Ella will be surprised."

Addie folded the material and put it in her dress pocket "Thanks, Lottie. See you for lunch on Friday."

Her friend smiled as she watched Addie head for the big white house that sat on the rise.

The truck carrying stock drove back to the field where the hired men had gathered to help unload the animals into a corral near the barn. Addie watched from the office window. The men held wide gates on each side of the truck so the animals couldn't escape. When the back gate of the truck was opened the mass burst forth. The bull was a different story. The men had to prod him with poles they stuck through the slats on the truck. He threw up his head and kicked up his heels as he lunged from the truck. He was solid black, big and mean. Caleb was standing in the corral when the bull rushed out. He scampered onto the fence as the men hurried to close the gates.

Addie continued to watch and saw the cows crowded into a corner while the bull, in another fenced area, continued his antics before settling down.

She saw Caleb approach the driver and check over papers. He must have been satisfied because the truck lumbered back to the drive, its big rubber tires grinding away.

Caleb came to the office an hour later. "Hi, Addie."

"Hi, Caleb. Was the delivery satisfactory?"

"The count was right. I don't know if Alex plans on breeding that stock or not. That's one mean bull he bought. If he's out in the field, all you gals better keep an eye out if you go out walkin'. I don't trust him."

"What does Alex need with another bull?"

Caleb offered a sly smile. "Well now, Addie. There's only so many ladies one bull can service."

Addie felt her face burn. Caleb caught her embarrassment and his smile became a wide grin. "This one comes from good stock. Alex wants bigger and better animals."

He handed the papers to Addie. "I don't know how you keep track of all this stuff."

"That's why I went to school. I know how to do the paperwork and you know how to run the farm. Are your hired men working out?"

He nodded his head. "I could use a couple more hands. Jess talks about goin' back to Oklahoma but I think it's just talk. I know he don't like livin' with the other two men. Maybe that's part of it."

"I don't blame him. Jess is cleaner, smarter and quieter. I often wonder what is going on behind those dark deep-set eyes of his. Why don't you sit down, Caleb?"

"No thanks, Lottie will have my supper on the table. You know, Addie, I've been thinkin'. There's that little place down near the creek that ain't bein' used for anythin'. I wonder if Alex would let Jess fix that place up. That would get him his own spot."

Apparently Caleb has given this careful thought.

"I don't see why not. I'll ask him when he comes out this weekend. Is Jess going to the cinema with us on Saturday?"

"Said he would," he answered.

CHAPTER 16

Saturday was a pleasant day for the end of August. Addie was up early. She opened the shutters and let the eastern sun flood the room. A faint smile appeared as she watched particles of dust float through the beaming rays. It's like dancing, she thought, as she allowed a fairy tale picture to cloud her mind, but not for long. Ella dropped a pot on the kitchen floor with a big bang which brought Addie back from the dream state.

Alex was due to arrive at nine. He always waited to have breakfast at the farm because he preferred Ella's cooking, and it saved him money. Addie had a cup of coffee. She waited until he came to eat because that was the time they used to catch up on the week's farm activities.

They sat at the dining room table. Alex was in a good mood. "I'm eager to see the new stock. I'll have calves in the spring, and I can sell some of the older cattle to the government this fall. The price is going up every day."

Addie was pouring syrup on pancakes. "Caleb said we should be cautious around the new bull. I told Ella to be watchful if she goes out near the barn."

Ella had prepared eggs, pancakes and ham. She also fried doughnuts and shook them in powdered sugar which she brought into the room along with an enamel coffee pot. "More coffee?" she asked.

Alex shook his head.

"None for me," answered Addie. "Will you be ready to go this evening?"

"Yes, ma'am. I'm so lookin' forward to it I can hardly stand still. I'll feed Mr. Alex his dinner and clean up when we get back, if that is all right."

"That will be fine," said Addie.

Alex cleared his throat.

Had she overstepped? Addie tried to cover her mistake. "Is that acceptable to you, Alex?"

"Nice that you recognized I was here." Then he nodded his agreement.

Ella placed the doughnuts on the table, quietly turned, and went back to the kitchen.

He finished the last bite of ham on his plate before asking, "Do you want to accompany me to the barn to look over the new stock or have you already seen them?"

The invitation was unexpected. In the three months Addie had been there Alex had never asked her to go with him to see the animals or anywhere else on the farm. Why would these cattle be any different?

But, she wasn't going to let the invitation pass. "I would," she answered.

Addie placed a straw hat on her head and tied it under her chin. Alex grabbed his Panama hat. They left by the kitchen door. Ella sat in a chair under the roof on the back of the house while she shucked ears of popcorn.

"We are going to check out the new stock," she said to Ella. Why she felt the maid needed to know, she wasn't sure.

Ella looked up and smiled. "I went on down to look at them. They're a mixed up bunch."

Addie could smell the animals before they reached the fenced in area where the cattle remained.

Alex explained. "I've got forty head that I'll need to feed through winter. If my bulls perform the way I expect, I'll have forty new calves in the spring." Alex leaned his arm on the top board of the fence but Addie had to climb up on the first slat. Ella was right. The animals were a mixture of colors: black, red, some with white faces, many with various white spotting, with and without horns. The bull was pure black with horns that looked as mean as he did. Each head of cattle was heavy weighing between four hundred and six hundred pounds.

Alex explained, "These came out of southern Virginia from a line started in Herfordshire, England in the 1700's by a man named Benjamin Tompkins. They are a cross between Herefords and Aberdeen Angus. Good meat cattle and the government will need it. In October I'm selling off the other stock I've got."

Addie turned and looked at him. "Why did you ask me to come and look at these cows?"

"Because I have information from the West Virginia Research people on feeding and you are going to have to help sort it out for Caleb. He has to figure out how much and what mixture to feed these girls. Seeing them first-hand you can understand the importance of proper feeding."

Her eyes opened wide. "You expect me to do that?"

"I'll help you. It's a matter of math regarding the portions per animal."

She stepped off the fence. "I thought you just feed animals hay and corn silage in the winter."

"If I am going to have a successful farm, then I need to approach it in a scientific manner. If I can get a good line going, people will be coming to me to buy breeding stock in the future."

Alex turned and they began walking back to the house. "Are Caleb and Jess going to the picture show this evening?" he asked.

"Yes. There will be five of us. Want to come along?"

He looked over at her and smiled. "No thanks. I'll keep the light burning until you and Ella return."

"Alex, you need to get away from your law practice and this farm. All of your days are tied up. You don't seem to make time to enjoy yourself."

"What makes you think I am not enjoying my life?"

"I'll be honest." She stopped walking and faced him squarely. "Because you are not the same person I met in Colorado."

A shadow fell over his face. "Perhaps I'm not. Things are different here. You must understand that. I would like very much to attend the cinema with all of you, but I can't risk the stories that will filter down the line."

His explanation did not set well with Addie. "Risk it. Play the generous employer who is taking his help out for a well-deserved evening. Everyone would say how lucky we are to be working for you."

They assumed their walk toward the house. "I could just give you the money to pay for the tickets."

"That's not the same as going to the ticket window, buying the tickets and handing them to each one of us. You would look like a benevolent soul and gain stature."

"And make Caleb and Jess feel small in the process. I'm not that kind of a person, and I hope you don't think I am."

Irritation was building in them both causing Addie to apologize. "I'm sorry, Alex. I didn't mean it to sound that way. I would like to see you less concerned. The farm is doing well, and you said you are winding down your law practice. What else is bothering you?"

His voice was kind. "I'm fine, Addie. I believe a night out is going to be a good time for all of you. I will be quite happy catching up on some reading."

Alex went upstairs when they reached the house and Addie went to her room before getting ready for the evening ahead.

Addie looked in the mirror one more time before she left to find Ella. Her high cheekbones had a touch of color from the sun. The bobbed hairdo was growing longer. She had snipped the bangs and snipped here and there so her honey-colored hair still looked presentable. A touch of Vaseline to her eyebrows seemed to enhance her hazel eyes.

She wore a camisole under the airy beige shirtwaist Lottie had made and it looked nice with the navy skirt she wore. The day was still warm but it might be cool as the evening wore on so she carried a fringed white shawl. Once again, she checked her small purse to be sure it held a handkerchief and twenty cents for two tickets. She had a nickel and one quarter left from her last month's pay. Begrudgingly, she dropped them into her purse in the event of an unforeseen emergency.

Ella was standing in the kitchen chewing her nails.

"You look very nice," complimented Addie.

Ella wore a calico dress with the lace kerchief around her neck. The ends were pinned together in front with a small pin in the shape of a flower. "Thank you, Miss Addie. It was right nice of you and Miss Lottie to give this to me. I don't think I've ever had anythin' so pretty. I'm jumpy as a cat."

That was obvious to Adelaide. She looked at the attractive young girl who was completely unaware of her outward beauty. "We are going to have a good time. Did you get Mr. Alex his dinner?"

"Yes, ma'am. I even had time to clean up the dishes. He don't eat a whole lot, so it was easy."

They heard the carriage, with covered top, coming up the lane. "Be sure and bring a shawl because it might be a cool ride on the way back," advised Addie.

Caleb and Jess were in the front seat with Caleb driving. Lottie sat in the back and shifted to the corner so Addie and Ella could fit on the seat with her. Jess hopped his tall, well-muscled frame down from the carriage to give them a hand up. Addie wasn't prepared for how snappy he looked. Jess was dressed in black hat, shirt and trousers with a silver band around his tall hat and a polished silver belt buckle on the belt at his waist. A wide smile brightened his handsome, dusky face. "Evenin', ladies," he said as his strong, work-worn hand helped them onto the step of the carriage.

"Good evening," replied Addie. "It looks like it will be a pleasant night."

The usually quiet Jess was vocal this evening. "It does. You three ladies look so well-done-up Caleb and I are proud to tote you to town. Right Caleb?" Jess climbed up and took his seat.

Caleb turned and gave an appreciative smile to the three young ladies. "That we are!"

Lottie was wearing the new dress she had made. She wore the gold locket her parents had given her, and a wide-brimmed straw hat trimmed with narrow blue and white ribbon streamers. Her plump face appeared to have a special glow. "You two look very nice. I don't think I've been dressed up for a year or more," she said.

"Whoever thought going to a picture show could be this exciting?" said Addie. "Did you bring a shawl?" she asked Lottie.

"I don't think we'll need one, but I packed mine behind the seat. We should put yours and Ella's back there and save the bother of carrying them."

"We can do that once we get to town. We'll get mussed up trying to do it now," answered Addie.

Lottie looked over at Ella. "What do you think, Ella?"

She gripped her shawl with two hands. "I'm fine, jus' fine."

"This is Ella's first trip to the cinema," informed Addie.

"Do you think a movie about the war is a good introduction to a picture show? Maybe we should have waited for a funny one," suggested Lottie.

"Lottie Bell! You and I both agreed that it didn't matter what was playing," said an irked Adelaide. "It's called "The American Girl" so it could be about a romance during the war."

Lottie rolled her eyes. "It could be but I doubt it."

The carriage had turned onto the main drive. Addie glanced at the house to see if Alex was watching them leave or give them a wave of his hand. He was nowhere in sight. She breathed an inward sigh. He was not even interested enough to say goodbye.

But, Alex was watching from the office window. Watching as the young set rode away and wishing he could be with them.

CHAPTER 17

Alex was finishing breakfast when Adelaide came into the dining room. He looked up and smiled. "How was your evening out?" he asked.

"Happy and sad," she replied.

He rose from his chair to pull out a chair for her to sit at the table. "What kind of an answer is that?"

Addie took the seat and Alex went back to his place.

Adelaide poured a cup of coffee from an earthen pot on the table. It was still hot. There were pieces of cheese and a plate of blackberries on the table; she began nibbling.

Looking over at Alex, she replied, "The happy part was the ride to and from. We sang, played guessing games and tried to count the stars in the sky. It was such a lovely evening. The picture show was the sad part. An American girl was in love with a German-American boy who was sent by his father to Europe to serve in the German army. She went to France to visit her aunt. The boat she was on was torpedoed by the Germans. She survived that, only to discover her aunt was dead when she reached France. Rather than return to America she stayed on to nurse wounded French soldiers. German soldiers came with the intention of violating the French women. Her German boyfriend finds her and saves her only to be arrested and both are sentenced to be shot. They are saved in the end."

She spread her hands. "There you have it in a nutshell. I can't say it was an uplifting moving picture. I was on edge through the whole film. I hope it didn't scare Ella away from the cinema. She sat next to me and cried most of the time. When she wasn't crying, she gripped my arm so hard I have her fingernail prints to prove it. She was silent the whole trip back."

He grinned. "I believe the picture is one I can do without."

Ella came into the room. "Miss Addie. I didn't know you was up. I got ham and eggs."

"I would like a piece of toast. Ella, I hope you weren't so upset about that film last night that you weren't able to sleep."

Ella perked up. "Oh, Miss Adelaide, I fell right to sleep. That movin' picture was so excitin' I can't wait to go again!"

After Ella left, Alex laughed aloud. "Adelaide, you may have unearthed a part of Ella we didn't know existed."

"Jess was surprising. He kept us laughing with his remarks. Maybe it was just because it was good to laugh after seeing that picture. He and Caleb are a good pair."

Then she remembered. "Caleb wondered if Jess could fix up that little cabin down near the creek. He said Jess isn't pleased living with those other two hired men."

111

"Why?" That's a good house they're in. They each have their own space."

"They share the living area and kitchen. Jess is a cut above those two."

He raised an eyebrow. "You've noticed?"

She looked over her coffee cup at him. "Don't tell me you haven't."

A light grin appeared. "Of course I have. He's welcome to fix up that place if he wants to."

"Don't forget to tell Caleb when you see him. I told him I would ask you."

Alex got up from his chair. "I'll leave that up to you. I worked on the feeding portions last evening and I want to go over them with you. Come to the office when you're finished. I'm going back to town as soon as we check over the figures."

A half-hour later Addie met him in the office. He had a typed copy of a schedule he had received from the West Virginia Research people.

"This shows how important it is to get the right balance of moisture, protein, fat, carbohydrate and fiber to raise cattle that are well-fleshed out but not overly fat. We've got the corn silage, timothy and rye hay, and the wheat straw. We will have to find a source for the soybean hay and cottonseed meal."

Addie looked over the sheet. "Where are you going to store this? The barn is full of the hay and straw."

"This is my idea." He pulled out another sheet of paper. "The men can build a big lean-to next to the barn and divide it into bins. You will

112

have to do some searching to find what we need. I'm sure there are places farther south where we can get the cottonseed meal and have it shipped up by train. I'm not sure about the soybean hay. We may be able to substitute clover for that."

Addie had been standing and looking over Alex's shoulder. She moved to the arm chair next to the desk. "How do you expect me to get this information?"

Alex leaned back in the desk chair. "You can write to the Department of Agriculture in Washington and get some answers."

"Can't you ask someone who is a successful farmer?"

He contemplated her question. "I suppose I can, but I'm not sure they are scientifically up to date."

Addie chuckled. "Most likely not in Clarke County."

"We raise some of the best horses and dairy cows in the country," he countered.

"We're not talking horses or dairy cows, Alex. We are talking about a special breed of cattle that you are pinning your hopes on. I will do my best."

He seemed to relax. "I know you will. Once you find out some information let me know right away. Meanwhile, I'll talk with Caleb and see what we need to do about getting a storage place ready."

He rose from the chair. "You are not to work in the office today. It's a beautiful Sunday. Let's see if we can find Caleb and get his ideas about what I have in mind."

"Be sure and bring the sketch. I'm going to get my notebook and pencil."

"You're not going to need those," Alex said.

Addie was of a different opinion. "I believe I am. When the job is completed there might be a difference of opinion of what you wanted and how Caleb understands it. I can pull out these notes and save a lot of hard feelings. I'm sure you recall the argument about the horse stalls."

He gave an embarrassed grin. "That wasn't my finest hour. I'll wait for you out back."

They found Caleb at home finishing breakfast. Lottie came to the door.

"Good morning," she greeted them. "I see you survived last night's outing."

Addie laughed. "Ella says she can't wait to go again."

"Good morning, Lottie," said Alex. "I have some business to discuss with Caleb."

"Hi Alex. Come in and have a seat."

"This must be mighty important," remarked Caleb.

It was the first time Alex had been inside the house since they moved in, but he came in and sat down as though he owned the place, which he did. Lottie cleared off the remainder of the breakfast dishes and all four sat at the table.

Alex unfolded his packet of papers.

"Alex is getting scientific," joshed Addie.

He just looked at her.

She quickly lifted the flap on her notebook and prepared to take notes.

Alex went over the information he had gathered about his idea of how they should store and mix the fodder. After some speculations they settled on a plan that satisfied both of them. Caleb would figure out the supplies needed and Addie would order them. It was a project that couldn't wait.

Lottie sat quietly as the men talked and watched Addie take notes.

When the conversation was finished, Caleb walked to the door with Alex.

Lottie remained as Addie reviewed what she had written before she folded up her notebook.

"Addie, that was beautiful."

"Beautiful?" questioned a puzzled Adelaide.

"The way you took the notes. Getting that training was perfect for you. I am happy that you decided to do that. You have always had a good mind, and I think you are going to be more satisfied as a secretary than as a teacher. Even if it takes you away from here."

"Lottie, why would you say something like that?"

"It's a feeling I have."

Addie whispered, "I think carrying that new little Dunn around is affecting you."

Lottie laughed, "Maybe so."

Alex called, "Are you ready to head back, Adelaide?"

"Coming," she answered.

They were on their way back to the house when he asked, "Have you seen the whole place?"

Addie shook her head. "I have not ventured farther than Lottie's and the barn."

"I'm going riding this afternoon. Would you like to go?"

This invitation was unexpected. "I haven't been on a horse since I lived at home and they were not the quality of horse that you have here."

"Jess can pick out one that you would be comfortable on."

He didn't need to ask again. "I would love to, but I don't have riding clothes."

"I'll lend you a pair of my riding pants."

"Then I guess I can't refuse."

She only had to draw the waist in a few inches with a belt and roll up the legs of the riding pants a few turns. She wore a plaid long-sleeved shirt and flat oxford shoes. Her reflection in the mirror was far from attractive, but she was not going to pass up this chance to spend time with Alex alone. She tied on her wide-brimmed straw hat and declared herself ready.

Alex laughed when he saw her.

"Don't embarrass me any more than I feel embarrassed," she advised.

"I think you look cute."

She sent a wry smile in his direction.

They walked out to the stables and found Jess saddling her horse. He looked up as they approached and grinned widely when he saw Addie.

"I swear, Miss Adelaide, you sure do look cute in those duds."

"They are not to my liking, but they will have to do."

"I saddled up Chessie for you. He behaves well and he's got spirit if you need it."

"I doubt I'll need spirit. I haven't been on a horse in almost three years. It will take me a while to get acclimated," she told him.

Jess gave Addie a boost up into the saddle.

Alex stood next to the horse she was seated on. "How do you feel?"

"High and shaky," she replied.

"Do you want to change your mind?"

"No. I'll get the feel of it once we start out."

Addie was surprised at the vast expanse of the place. It was no wonder they could grow crops, raise horses and cattle on the land. It was little wonder Caleb said he needed more hired help. It must be a challenge just to keep up with what needed to be done, thought Addie.

They rode side by side at a leisurely pace.

"If my cattle turn out the way I hope, I will concentrate on them and give up the horses. James Anderson advised that it is better to raise either than to raise both."

"You love the horses. How can you give them up?"

"I will keep a few for pleasure," he responded. "My horse needs exercising. Do you mind if I leave you to run him a bit?"

117

"No," she answered even though she did mind. "I know the way back to the stable."

Without fanfare, he was off in a gallop leaving Addie to watch him go. This ride wasn't as enjoyable as she thought it would be, and hardly worth the lameness and aches she would feel from riding a horse once again.

Jess was at the stable when she arrived. "Have a good ride?"

"I saw the whole place."

"Where's the boss?"

"Boss? Oh, you mean Alex. I've never heard him called boss before. He took his horse for some exercise."

"Don't think I would have left a good-lookin' lady like you to ride back alone. C'mon, I'll help you down."

She swung her leg over the saddle and fell back into Jess's strong arms saving her from landing on her bottom.

"Oh, my goodness!" she exclaimed. "I guess I'm not as agile as I thought I was."

His face was close to hers and she could feel his warm breath and the resonance of his voice. "I'll catch you any time you need me."

Addie was unnerved causing her to be awkward in getting her feet stabilized. Jess continued to hold onto her until he was sure she was on solid ground. She hadn't expected the reaction she felt from being held by Jess. She mumbled a clumsy thank you and went to the house.

CHAPTER 18

Friday of the next week Addie and Lottie were taking their mothers to visit Aunt Lilly in Boyce. Jess had the horse harnessed and hitched to the same conveyance they had taken to the picture show. He stood next to the rig in the front drive. Lottie had not yet arrived, but Addie decided to go outside and wait for her.

"Big day planned?" asked Jess.

"Lottie and I are going to take our mothers to visit my aunt. I should have been down there long before this. I didn't find the time."

He leaned on the carriage. "Sometimes you have to make time for what's important."

"You know how busy it is around here. We were fortunate to get that evening out at the cinema."

His clean-shaven face showed a sly grin. "Want to go again?"

The casual question threw her off. She fussed with her hat and didn't look at him. "Ella is all for it."

He stepped away from the carriage and she could smell a freshly laundered shirt mixed with the musky odor of recent labor. "I don't mean Ella. I mean you and me."

She felt so inept. "I don't...I don't think we could."

"Why couldn't we?"

"What I meant to say is that I don't think we should."

"Why shouldn't we? Unless you're ashamed to be seen with me."

"That isn't true!" she answered.

"Good. We'll plan on next Friday evening. Here comes Lottie. I hitched up a good horse for you so you shouldn't run into any problems." He didn't leave an opening for Addie to refuse before he turned and headed in the direction of the barn.

Addie watched the tall, strong, former cowboy saunter off and saw him tip the brim of his hat as he passed Lottie.

She was carrying a picnic basket. "Jess seems to be in a happy mood. I brought some cookies for your aunt's family and also for us to eat if we get hungry."

"Jess just asked me to go to the cinema with him next Friday evening," said a dazed Adelaide.

"Well, I'll be. What did you say?"

Addie threw up her hands. "Nothing. He didn't give me a chance to answer."

"Are you going to go?"

"I don't know. I don't even know him very well."

Lottie put the picnic basket on the floor of the carriage. "Go to the moving picture and you'll get to know him a lot better."

Addie walked over to the driver's side and climbed up. "You're full of advice."

Lottie pulled herself up into the seat. "He wouldn't be Caleb's friend if he wasn't a decent sort. Caleb told Jess that Alex said he could fix up that little cabin by the Buckmarsh Run and Caleb said he hasn't heard him say much about going back to Oklahoma. Could be he sees something around here more interesting," she teased.

"Stop, Lottie. It could be that Jess is lonesome and wants company."

"Your company," she said and laughed at her own frivolity.

Addie gave her a disgusted look. "Your mother knows we're coming, doesn't she?"

"I assume your mother told her after Alex gave her the message. If not, it will only take her a minute or two to be ready."

"How do you know that?"

"Because I know my mother. She likes to get out of the house."

Addie chucked to the horse and they were on their way that early September morning.

When they reached the farm where their parents lived, Addie was surprised to see Mrs. Foster and her mother waiting on the porch. They left the porch as soon as they saw the carriage.

Addie hopped off to help them into the back seat. "Momma, I expected to drive over and pick you up."

"It is a pretty morning for a walk. Chip offered to watch Sarah Jane so that gives me some freedom."

121

"Doesn't Chip have school?" asked Adelaide.

"Not today. All the teachers had a meeting to attend."

Laura Richards climbed up into the buggy and took her seat next to Mrs. Foster. "Chip is doing well in school, Adelaide. He has decided to stay and finish high school."

Addie returned to the driver's seat. "I'm thankful for that. He talked of quitting."

"That would be a mistake," enjoined Lottie's mother. "Chip is a smart young man." Then she changed the subject. "Do you know that I have only met your Aunt Lilly once, Adelaide? That was seven years ago when we first moved here. I hope she doesn't mind Lottie and me tagging along."

The carriage creaked down the lane until they came to the main road. "I telephoned Aunt Lilly. She is happy we're coming. You know, Momma? I was glad I spent that summer down there. I think it helped me find direction in my life."

"It wasn't the direction I wanted, but it seems to be working out," answered Laura.

Still a stab of regret in those words, thought Addie.

They rode through Berryville and onto the pike that led the six miles to Boyce. Outside of town, Addie let the horse go at a faster pace.

"You know, Momma," Adelaide called over the clip-clop of the horse's hooves. "Uncle Frank put in the telephone because he thought it was good for his business."

"That would have to be the reason," said her mother. "He's too tight-fisted otherwise."

Lottie spoke up, "I haven't met either your aunt or your uncle, but you did bring your little cousins by when I worked for Miss Butler. They were another reason I brought the cookies."

"It's good you did. I didn't think to bring anything. My mind gets so tied up with the farm business that sometimes I don't think of anything else."

"How is the farm doing?" asked Mrs. Foster.

"Very well. Alex has purchased a new breed of cattle he wants to raise. Caleb is getting his plans in order to build a big grain area because Alex has read how important it is to get the right mixture of nutrients to feed them."

"You and Alex seem to be working closely," her mother remarked.

"It is necessary," answered Addie.

"Just remember who you are," said Laura.

Addie and Lottie exchanged a tired look.

When they reached the Pierce home, Lilly ran out to meet them with CJ in her arms. Adelaide noticed immediately that he still looked unhealthy.

Although there was a two-year age difference between the two sisters, Lilly appeared younger. She was slim and tall like Laura but her body did not show the signs of hard work that Laura's did. Perhaps it was worth it to be married to a man with a healthy income, even though he was a blowhard.

Lilly was all a twitter, "Come in, come in. Mrs. Foster, how nice to see you once again, and this must be your daughter, Lottie, whom I have heard so much about."

Addie finished securing the horse to a post before she came around to greet her aunt. "Hi, Aunt Lilly."

Her aunt embraced her with one arm while she held CJ in the other. "Adelaide. My, you look so grown up. How was school and your position on the farm, and…oh, we have so much to talk about. I have lunch ready. I hired one of the local ladies to help and she has outdone herself."

The four visitors followed their hostess into the house. "Addie, you go ahead and show the ladies where they can freshen up. I'm sure it was a bothersome ride."

Lilly went to the kitchen to talk with her helper.

When they were all seated at the dining room table, Aunt Lilly said grace, "We thank you for our family and visitors. We ask you to bless this food and all who are present. Please watch over Laura, Mrs. Foster, Adelaide and Lottie Bell for a safe journey home. Amen."

"Amen."

Lilly's helper placed a tureen of bean soup on the table which Aunt Lilly dished out. That was followed by a variety of sandwiches, deviled eggs, and a gelatin salad. Dessert was a crème brulee.

"This is a French dessert," informed Aunt Lilly. "I guess if the French are our friends during this war, we should learn more of their culture."

It tasted much like custard with a caramel sauce to Adelaide.

"Alex has had men from the government come to the farm. Because of the war, the farms should prosper. There isn't one thing on the place that the government isn't buying. It should help Uncle Frank, and also the farm where Momma and Pa live."

"That doesn't necessarily mean that it will help those of us who work the farm," replied her mother.

"Tell us about your school, Adelaide" encouraged Aunt Lilly as a way of easing the conversation.

Addie was more than happy to expound on what she had learned until CJ could be heard waking up from his nap.

Lilly rose from her chair. "Excuse me, please. I don't let CJ cry."

"How is he doing?" asked Laura.

"What we hoped was curable turns out to be more serious. He has a heart problem. Dr. Hawthorne says he may not be with us too much longer, so we make each day special until the Lord calls him home."

"Oh Lilly, I am so sorry. I didn't know." And the otherwise stoic Laura burst into tears.

Then Mrs. Foster pulled out a handkerchief and started sniffling. Lottie looked at Addie with a lost look and Adelaide wasn't sure how to react.

Addie swallowed a lump in her throat. "Is there anything we can do?" she asked.

"Love him and enjoy him as we do. Frank and I are resigned to the inevitable. Now, I must go in and get him."

Laura rose from her chair and followed her sister.

Mrs. Foster dabbed at her eyes. "It is so difficult to lose a child. Lottie should have a sister, but when she was born it wasn't to be."

Lottie's eyes opened wide. "You never told me that, Momma."

"There was no need. We have to shoulder our disappointments."

Laura and Lilly came back with CJ. The frail two year-old was smiling, content in his mother's arms.

Adelaide was concerned. "Are you sure there is nothing that can be done?"

Lilly shook her head. "Let's not dwell on our misfortunes and spoil the day. Haven't we had a wonderful visit?"

They had to admit that was true.

They heard a ruckus as Emily and Flossie burst into the room.

Addie rose as soon as they entered.

"We came home from school as fast as we could. Momma told us you would be here," and they ran to Adelaide and hugged her as tight as they could.

"I haven't seen you girls in two years. You have gotten taller and prettier." She kissed each one on the cheek.

"Say hello to your Aunt Laura, girls," said their mother.

"Hi, Aunt Laura, Hi, Miss Lottie," they responded in unison.

"This is Mrs. Foster, Miss Lottie's mother," informed Lilly.

"Hello, Mrs. Foster," they said in a calmer voice.

"I am very glad to meet you," she answered.

"I brought some sugar cookies," Lottie said. "Will it be all right for the girls to have one?"

"How thoughtful," said Lilly. "The girls are always starved when they get home from school. Girls, go wash your hands and bring in a glass of milk to have with your cookie."

They eagerly went to the kitchen to do as their mother asked.

Mrs. Foster exclaimed, "My goodness, I almost forgot. I brought you a little something. I hope it isn't squashed." She reached into her tote bag and pulled out a small paper bag and peeked inside before she breathed a sigh of relief. She handed the bag to Lilly.

Lilly reached in and pulled out a small plant of ivy.

"It could use some water," Mrs. Foster apologized.

"It is lovely, and I shall place it on the windowsill in the kitchen. It will be a bright spot when winter sets in. Thank you."

Lottie's mother was beaming.

The visitors prepared to leave with everyone in a relaxed mood. The shadow of CJ's ill health had been pushed aside.

Lilly and the girls stood outside of the big farmhouse and waved as the carriage went down the long drive.

CHAPTER 19

The supplies for the feed bins had arrived and the men were in the process of erecting the tall, wide storage structure close to the barn. With the help of the Department of Agriculture, Addie had located a place that would ship the cottonseed meal Alex wanted, but she had yet to find a source for soybean hay.

She was looking out the office window when she saw Jess in the fenced area near the barn. She knew he would expect to go to the cinema, which would be in three days, even though she hadn't agreed. Addie hadn't seen Jess since that brazen moment he asked her to go and hadn't given her a chance to respond. It was a pleasure to watch the fluid motion of his agile body as he guided the animals into their enclosure. Jess was separating the cows from the bull and the gate was almost shut then the bull wheeled. He kicked up his hind legs and caught the unsuspecting cowhand with his powerful hooves. Jess crumbled in a heap.

Addie ran from the house, screaming to Caleb on the way. He was at Jess's side by the time she reached the spot. The other two hired men kept the bull at bay until Caleb could manage to move Jess out of danger.

Fear for his friend caused the color to drain from Caleb's face. "Addie, go to the house and bring a heavy quilt. We've got to get him to a bed."

Addie ran as fast as she could. She returned with a quilt and saw Ella holding another blanket. Caleb had the men bring a flat of boards they had nailed together. Being as careful as they could, they moved Jess onto the quilt. Grabbing the corners of the quilt, they were able to pull the injured and unresponsive man onto the flat board.

"Take him to the house and put him in my bed," Addie ordered. "Ella, put the blanket over him. I'll run on ahead and call Dr. Hawthorne."

Jess's dusky face was an ashen gray. The men transferred him to Addie's bed where they stared down at him as if in a stupor and not knowing what to do. There was nothing they could do but wait for Dr. Hawthorne, who was on his way.

Addie took charge. "You hired men can go back to your duties. Caleb, you had better go and tell Lottie what has happened."

He declined. "I'll stay and keep an eye out for the doctor."

Jess's skin was cold and clammy, his breathing shallow. Addie knew how to feel for a pulse. It was weak and thready. She lifted the blanket to see where the bull had struck him. There were dirt marks on Jess's torn shirt but little blood. With all her heart she prayed the doctor would get here soon.

It was a long twenty-five minutes before she heard the Model T's engine sputter to a stop.

Caleb was there to meet the physician and usher him in to where the previously robust young man lay motionless.

The doctor acknowledged Addie with a nod and went to the patient's side. "Cut his shirt sleeve," he ordered as he opened his bag and drew out a stethoscope and leather cuff.

Addie had pulled a pair of scissors from a side table and slit the shirt sleeve. She watched as the physician put the cuff around Jess's upper arm and placed his stethoscope below that to listen. Then he pulled out a hypodermic syringe, filled it with medicine from a vial and injected it into Jess's other arm.

"He's in shock." He addressed Caleb. "Bring in that low bench I saw on the porch. We'll raise the foot of the bed up onto it."

Addie heard Caleb call to the hired men as he went to get the bench. The foot-tall bench was hauled into the room where the four men lifted the end of the bed and placed the legs of the bed onto the bench.

The doctor took Jess's blood pressure once again before he started to examine the injured man. Adelaide thought he should have done so in the first place. As though sensing her thoughts, the good doctor said, "We have to try to get his system working first."

He had Addie cut off the rest of the sweat-soaked shirt. She noticed Jess's side was turning black and blue, and the physician carefully felt the injured area. "He has broken ribs. I'm not sure how

131

many. I'd like to get him up to the hospital for an x-ray but it isn't wise to move him."

"He is going to recover isn't he?" asked a worried Adelaide.

"I've given him some stimulant medication. He's young and strong. There's a danger of internal bleeding and a punctured lung. At this point, I believe I can rule the lung out."

Dr. Hawthorne took Jess's blood pressure again. "It's coming up. That's good."

A few minutes later, Jess began to moan.

The physician checked his blood pressure once again and was satisfied with the result. "I believe I can rule out the internal bleeding."

Caleb hadn't left. He was sitting in a corner chair without saying a word when a concerned Lottie came hustling into the room. He got up to meet her. "I was going to come to the house and tell you."

"I heard the shouting and commotion and knew something was wrong."

Caleb put his arm around his wife. "I think he's going to be all right."

"Thank God," responded Lottie.

"Alex should never have bought that bull," said Addie.

"Now, don't blame this on Alex," said a level-headed Caleb. "Accidents happen on a farm. This has taught us to have two men present when we have to deal with that bull. Lottie, you stay on here and help if they need it. I'll tend to the hired men." He kissed his wife on the cheek and left.

Dr. Hawthorne took Jess's blood pressure and pulse. "We'll leave the bed with the foot elevated until I'm satisfied he is stabilized." He leaned his face close to Jess. "Can you hear me?" he asked.

Jess's dark eyelashes flickered as he struggled to open his eyes.

"Bring some hot coffee," Dr. Hawthorne told no one in particular.

Ella must have heard the request because she had a cup poured when Addie came into the kitchen.

Worry showed on Ella's face. "I hope Jess is goin' to be fine, Miss Addie."

"We hope so too. You can bring in some lunch for the three of us. I'm sure Dr. Hawthorne didn't have time to eat before he came."

Addie returned to her room to find Lottie sitting in the forner chair vacated by Caleb and Dr. Hawthorne by the bedside. She handed the cup of coffee to the doctor. He took another syringe from his bag and drew the coffee into it. Attached was a short rubber tube which he placed in Jess's mouth and pressed the plunger to release a small amount into the injured man's mouth. Jess swallowed.

"Another river crossed," exclaimed the physician and proceeded to empty the syringe little by little into his patient's mouth.

"I have asked Ella to bring in lunch for us. I was sure you didn't have time to eat before you came," Addie said to the physician.

133

"I could use a bite," he confessed. "A glass of water would be appreciated also."

Addie's sitting room was adjacent to her bedroom. She and Lottie cleared off a small table where Ella could set the food. They placed a desk chair at the table for Dr. Hawthorne, while they chose to sit together on the upholstered settee. Jess's moan drifted into the room which brought a smile to their faces.

Ella carried in a tray of glasses and a pitcher of water. "I'll be back with the food." She exited the room quickly and returned with a platter of ham sandwiches, wedges of cheese, a plate of grapes and gingersnap cookies.

Addie left to inform Dr. Hawthorne that the lunch was ready.

At Jess's bedside, he turned and smiled. "Almost the whole cup. Once we're finished with lunch, you can have the men put the bed back on solid footing. I will have to shave his chest before I tape the rib cage. The tape will be uncomfortable when it's time to remove it and he won't appreciate pulling out hair along with it."

Addie looked down at Jess. His color had improved and his moans had increased. The thought of having to move him to tape his ribs did not appeal to her, but she knew she would have to help. Happenings of this kind had not occurred to her when she accepted the position of secretary and bookkeeper for Alex Lockwood. But, she was here and help was needed so there was no choice.

When they were finished eating, Lottie went to get Caleb and the hired men to reset the bed on the floor.

Addie picked up the scissors, pulled back the blanket. She gasped at the extent of the dark bruising covering his body bringing tears to her eyes. Addie covered her reaction by picking up the discarded shreds of his shirt and wadding them into a basket. She dabbed at her eyes and wiped her hands on her apron. Why was this affecting her so? Addie was a strong young woman and she needed to draw on that strength.

Caleb and the men arrived to reset the bed. Jess opened glazed eyes and looked around.

"You're in Addie's bed," informed Caleb. "That ol' bull almost did you in. The doc says you've got broken ribs so you're goin' to be out of commission for a while."

Jess didn't answer. He shut his eyes tight.

Once the bed was back on the floor, Dr. Hawthorne said, "You fellows can go. I'm going to tape up his chest now to make him more comfortable. He'll need plenty of rest while those ribs heal."

Caleb turned to his wife. "Lottie, I'll walk you back on home, if you're not needed here,"

"You go ahead," said Addie. "I'll send Ella over if I need anything."

Dr. Hawthorne shaved the dark hair on Jess's chest and cut strips of adhesive tape. Addie was called to the bedside where she was instructed to put one arm around Jess's neck and down his back while she reached the other around his waist and clasped her other hand. She rolled him slightly toward her and he groaned with pain. It was like cradling a baby, only this was a six-foot two-inch strapping man, his cheek resting on her arm and his face buried in her bosom. She prayed that the dazed Jess Edwards was not conscious of that fact.

When the doctor was through, he took pain pills from his bag and instructed Addie how to administer them. She knew quite a bit about medicine from working in the Davis drug store in Leadville.

"He's going to be suffering once he's fully alert. This medicine will take the edge off the discomfort. I'll be back in three days to see how he is doing. See that he drinks plenty of liquids in the meantime. For the next couple of days stay with tea, broth, coffee, water, and salty crackers."

Addie looked at the label on the bottle. Dilaudid. She knew the narcotic would help.

"Thank you, Dr. Hawthorne. Bring a bill when you return, I will pay you. I take care of Mr. Lockwood's affairs related to the farm."

"You are to call me if you have any concerns. We've pulled him out of grave danger. Now, if we can keep the pneumonia away, I feel it will be a matter of time and rest. Thank you for your help, Miss Richards."

"You're welcome," she answered, and watched from the doorway as the good doctor rattled off in his black Model T Ford leaving her alone to care for the injured Jess.

CHAPTER 20

The sun rising in the eastern sky gave Addie relief. It had been a long, anxious night. She had called Alex to tell him of Jess's misfortune and hoped he would hurry to her aid. But he said she had handled the situation well, and as he had an early court case in the morning, he would come as soon as he was through.

Did he not realize how the whole incident had drained her? He had rushed to her side when Lottie was so sick in Colorado. Why didn't he come now?

Addie had to readjust her thoughts or the irritation building within would explode into words better left unsaid once Alex arrived.

Jess had come in and out of lucidity. When he was awake he was in pain. She kept a cool cloth by the bedside and bathed his sweaty brow. The pain medicine was a help but it caused him to go into a deep slumber and she feared he wouldn't wake up. The long, lonely night had been agonizing for both of them.

Ella came into the room tiptoeing to where Addie sat. She whispered, "You want some breakfast, Miss Addie?"

"Just a cup of coffee, thank you."

"You look awful tired," said the young maid.

137

"I am. It has been a difficult night for Jess and for me. Perhaps I can get some sleep when Alex arrives."

"Maybe I should go get Miss Lottie," suggested Ella.

Jess's raspy voice cut the quiet of the room, "Get Caleb."

Ella jumped at the sound.

Addie startled and sprang to her feet. "You're awake," she said, and went to the bedside.

"Get Caleb." His voice was dry and hoarse.

"Is there something I can do?" she asked.

"No. Get Caleb, fast."

Ella flew out the door and met Caleb who was on his way up to the house. "Jess said you better come fast."

Caleb took off running and his long legs carried him at a fast pace. He was breathing heavily when he walked into Addie's room where he found her standing by the bed.

"Ella said Jess needs me."

"He asked for you," answered Addie.

Jess motioned with his finger for Caleb to lean down so he could whisper in his ear.

Caleb straightened with a face that was beet red. "Addie, this is a mite embarrassin', but he needs to relieve himself. Do you have a chamber pot handy?"

The color in her face matched Caleb's. "There's one right under the bed, but I don't know how you're going to be able to keep him from falling. He's weak and he can't move without excruciating pain."

"Send Ella for one of the other men," he ordered.

Before Addie could send Ella, she heard a car engine stop and Alex came bounding through the front door.

She ran to meet him. "Thank God you are here. Follow me. Caleb needs your help."

Addie left the room while the two men maneuvered Jess to his feet. She stood in the outer room and grit her teeth when she heard groans of pain. Minutes dragged like hours.

Alex came to her once the ordeal was finished. He put a protective arm around her. "I should have come last night. You sounded so confident and in control over the phone, I didn't realize the gravity of the situation."

She swallowed hard to relieve the lump in her throat. It wouldn't do to break down in tears. "How did you get here so soon this morning?"

"They rescheduled the court case. I am so sorry, Addie." He pulled her into his arms and held her tight. "It won't happen again. Whenever you need me, I promise to be right here."

The earlier irritation she had felt building toward Alex melted like ice on a warm day. She didn't want to move. The comfort of his arms held her spellbound until she heard Jess moaning.

"I need to give him some pain medicine," she said as she pulled away. "He has had a rough night."

"I believe you both have," Alex observed as he went with her to where Jess's face contorted from the raging pain.

She placed a pill in his mouth and braced his head with her hand so he could swallow water. Then she gently lay his head back on the pillow and wiped his brow with the cool cloth. "This will make you feel better."

Jess's answer was to take her hand in his. She left it there until he began to relax. Once his suffering had lessened, she patted his hand as though she were soothing a sick child.

Alex stood by and watched the scene with a discerning eye.

Addie came to where he stood. "The medicine will make him sleep."

"Have you had breakfast?" he asked her.

"No. Ella was going to bring me a cup of coffee only we got busy with Jess."

"I smell food," he said, "which means our little Ella is busy cooking our breakfast. I suggest that you freshen up. You and I will sit out at the table on the front porch and eat. Then, my dear girl, you are going to go to bed."

Addie smiled up at him. "That sounds like heaven," she answered.

After washing her hands and face and brushing her teeth, Adelaide felt better. She pulled a shawl around her shoulders, because the morning was cool, before meeting Alex on the porch.

Ella kept their plates of fried potatoes, eggs, sausage and grits warm in the oven. When she heard Addie go out the front door, she brought the breakfasts along with hot coffee.

Alex had seated Addie at the table for two.

He took his seat and addressed Ella. "Thank you. We will appreciate this food."

"Yes, sir. Do you need anything else?"

He looked over at Addie and smiled. "I have everything I want right here."

Addie was still fuzzy from the long night. If there was hidden meaning in his words, it was lost to her.

Alex spoke. "I'll get Lottie to come and sit with Jess while you get some rest."

"I don't want to bother Lottie, she has enough to do."

"Addie, you know that Lottie would be more than happy to help you out. You can't spend twenty-four hours a day with Jess," he said, with an edge to his voice.

She looked over at Alex. "I expect him to be doing better in a few days. The shock needs to wear off and then it will be a matter of getting his strength back. Jess is not one to wallow in being an invalid."

Alex took a bite of food. "You seem to know him well. You know, this will put me in a bind around the farm."

These words irked the tired Addie. "Are you upset that he was injured trying to handle that ugly bull you bought? I am sure no one is unhappier about what happened than he is. Don't sound selfish, Alex."

He was silent.

Addie held her coffee cup in her hand and looked out at the Blue Ridge Mountains. "Let's not spoil our morning. The view is exhilarating. Times like this I just want to let my mind wander and forget the rest of the world."

Alex pushed his empty plate aside. "You're right. You have a way of bringing me back to earth. Let's pretend we are at Caleb's shack in Colorado. Nothing but you, me and the water tumbling over the rocks as the stream makes its way down the mountain."

Addie smiled at the thought. "Carefree days. Where did they go so quickly? Now, I've put in a year of school, you're burdened with your law practice and this farm, Caleb and Lottie are married and expecting a baby in the spring…"

Alex came to attention. "What?"

Addie slapped a hand over her mouth. "That wasn't supposed to slip out."

"When did Lottie tell you?" he asked.

"Last month. Lottie hasn't told Caleb because she doesn't want him to worry. Don't you dare breathe a word of what I just told you. Lottie told me and Ella in confidence and here I betrayed her."

Alex rose from his chair. "Don't be so hard on yourself. Lawyers can keep secrets, and you're overtired. Go up and sleep in my bed. The sheets are clean."

She did not protest. "Wake me if Jess needs me. He can't have another pain pill for three hours."

Alex was clear with his response, "Ella and I will handle Jess. I have work to do in the office so we'll both be near."

"Be sure he has a blanket over him and wipe his brow if he needs it. He should have a drink of water if he wakes up."

Alex had heard enough. "Adelaide, get upstairs and get some rest."

She left the porch, went up the stairs and fell onto Alex's bed. The sheets smelled of fresh outdoor air. Then came the stirring realization that Alex always slept in this very spot. Twenty-year-old Adelaide Richards, secretary and bookkeeper for Lockwood farm, curled onto her side and fell fast asleep.

CHAPTER 21

Dr. Hawthorne arrived late in the morning four days later to find Addie and Jess having coffee on the front porch. He walked his portly but agile frame up the stone steps.

"Well, this is a surprise," he greeted Jess. "Four days ago I wasn't sure you would pull through. Sorry I'm a day late."

Jess offered a weak smile. "I never hurt so bad in my life, but I can't lay in that bed."

Addie rose to greet the physician. "Caleb helped him walk out here. Although Jess doesn't like to admit it, he is still very weak."

"I'll help you back in," said the doctor. "You are a fortunate young man."

"Yes, sir, I know I am. I've seen men die from lesser blows than that."

Dr. Hawthorne turned to Addie. "How are you holding up Miss Richards?"

She responded right away. "I was exhausted the first couple of days, but Alex stayed on. I would have been at a loss without him and Caleb. Would you like to have me send for Caleb?"

"Not necessary. If you will be kind enough to carry my bag, I believe I can help my patient back into the house without too much discomfort."

Addie noticed Jess set his face with resolve as the doctor assisted him to his feet. She knew every move was painful but the stoic Jess never flinched.

There was perspiration on his face when he lay back on the pillow. Addie picked up the cool cloth she kept at the bedside and wiped the moisture away.

Dr. Hawthorne took out his stethoscope and performed his examination. He listened to Jess's heart and had him take deep breaths to evaluate his lungs, but when he asked him to cough Jess refused.

"Sorry, Doc," he said. "I know what I can stand and I can't stand that."

The physician chuckled. "I am not surprised." He placed his stethoscope on Jess's abdomen and listened, then checked the injured rib area before placing the instrument back into his bag.

He stood back from the bed and talked to both Jess and Addie. "I'm satisfied. We have one more hurdle to jump. Pneumonia may set in. My recommendations are to walk three times a day, take deep breaths frequently, eat well and drink plenty of fluids. That regimen will help to stave it off."

He turned to Addie. "How much pain medicine do you have left?"

She handed him the bottle of pills. "If he has been getting them every three or four hours, stretch them to six and longer. I'll be back in a week. By then he should be down to one at bedtime."

"I have tried to not give them too often because they cause him to go into a deep slumber."

"Precisely the reason I want you to slack up on them. When he's sleeping he's not eating, drinking or moving," explained the doctor. "I want him to do all three."

He closed the hasps on his medical bag. "Give him a pain pill after I leave. I've worn him out for today. Keep up the good work and we'll get him back on his feet."

Addie nodded knowing it would be up to her to get Jess back on his feet.

She saw Dr. Hawthorne to the door and went back to her room where she bathed Jess's face. "Time for a pill." She placed the medicine in his mouth and raised his head with one hand. When she put the glass of water to his lips he placed his hand over hers. "Thanks, Addie. We've still got a date for the picture show."

She laughed and shook her head. "I never said I would go."

He offered a modest smile. "But, you will."

She remained in that spot until she felt him relax. He closed his coal-black eyes and began to drift off into another world.

Addie smiled down at the noble face that had lost its pinched expression. She slid her hand from beneath his. A night at the cinema was unlikely. But then, there was something appealing about the Oklahoma cowboy.

Addie checked the watch pin that Clayton Lockwood had given her. The feel of the ornate case caused her to think of Clay and wonder how he was. She hadn't received any news from him since he left for the military.

It was eleven o'clock before Addie could get into the office to finish some typing. She knew Caleb would come to check the figures for the feed mixtures because a load of soybean hay was coming in today. As the farmhands dumped feed in the middle of the enclosure for the animals, there was no way to tell how much each cow ate so Addie wasn't sure how Alex's scientific feeding was going to work out. Maybe it didn't make any difference as long as the cows all gained weight.

She wanted to go over and see Lottie after she finished in the office but she didn't want to leave Jess alone. Ella acted scared to death whenever Addie had asked her to sit with him for a short time. And Jess had remarked that he was better off by himself rather than to have Ella sitting straight as a poker and looking bug-eyed.

Two hours later, Addie was typing up a letter when Caleb came to the office. There was a wide grin on his face when he entered the open door.

"You look spritely," said Addie.

"I am. I'm gonna' be a daddy!"

"Caleb, that's wonderful. How is Lottie? I haven't seen her for almost a week."

"She is fine and dandy. I 'spect you heard that news before I did."

Addie turned away from the Royal type-writer. "What makes you say that?"

The lank and lean Caleb took a seat beside the desk. "Cause you didn't hop up and down and get all teary-eyed like most women."

Addie looked over teasingly and smiled. "I'm not like most women."

"That's true," he agreed.

"I don't know if that's a compliment or not."

"It's a compliment. Not many women measure up to you. But don't go gettin' your nose in the air just 'cuz I said so."

She chuckled. "There's not much danger in that. I know who I am. What can I help you with?"

"I need to go over that feed list again. They're bringin' the load of soybean hay today and I want to be sure I've got it right."

Addie pulled out a file drawer that contained the information. They were looking over the paper when they heard Jess call.

Caleb went in to see his friend with Addie following behind.

"I thought I heard your voice," said Jess. "I want to get out and see what's going on."

"You might be groggy from the medicine. I don't think it is a good idea," advised Addie.

Jess's words were sharp, "I'm asking Caleb."

Caleb eased the sting of that remark. "There's no call to get cranky, Jess. Guess it's a sign you're doin' better."

Jess was chagrined. "Sorry, Addie. There was no call for me to say that. I appreciate all you've done for me."

Addie came to the bedside. "I know you do. I believe it's because you are not the type of man who can lay around wallowing in self-pity."

"What have you got in mind?" asked Caleb.

"If I could get out there, I'd like to take a look at that cabin Alex said I could fix up. I figure by next week I should be able to get around by myself." Addie had placed a high-backed straight chair with the back to the side of the bed. Jess could grab onto the chair for leverage to raise himself up. It was a chore.

"Looks like you're not too ready for much," said Caleb. "Tell you what I'll do. We've got that low wagon out in the barn. I'll hitch up a pony to take you there."

"I'll lead the pony," interjected Addie. "I don't think this is a wise idea. If the pony gets frisky, the jarring could prove dangerous. What if the wagon overturns?"

"I've got to get out of this bed," said a determined Jess.

Addie decided it was best to go along with his want than to argue. "Caleb, stop by your house and ask Lottie if she will go with me when I drive Jess to the cabin. You have to stay around here for the load of soybean hay."

An hour later Caleb and Lottie arrived in the low wagon at the back door of the manor house.

149

Addie told Ella to put two quilts and pillows into the wagon. She gave Lottie a quick hug. "I haven't seen you all week. Why didn't you come by?"

"You said you would send Ella if you needed me. I thought it was best to stay away."

"You're right. Alex stayed for a couple of days and Caleb came by often."

"I think you saw more of Caleb than I did. He's satisfied that Jess is on the mend so maybe I'll get to see more of my husband again."

Addie laughed. "I couldn't handle Jess by myself. Come on in and see for yourself how he is progressing."

By the time they got into Addie's room the patient was on his feet with Caleb right next to him. Jess had on a blue denim shirt and leather jacket. Both the shirt and jacket had empty sleeves on the injured side. His tall cowboy hat sat atop his head.

Addie reached up and wiped his damp brow. "Are you sure you're up to this?" she asked.

"I can make it," he replied.

They settled Jess into the low bed of the wagon. Lottie sat on the seat and Addie took her place at the pony's head where she grabbed onto the bridle. "We're as ready as we'll ever be," she announced.

Caleb watched them go with a half-smile of worry on his weather-worn face.

They made slow progress to what once had been a decent log cabin. The metal roof needed a coat of paint, floor boards needed replacing, hinges on the door were rusting and the walls and windows needed caulking. The fireplace was in good shape but needed cleaning. The well was a few feet from the back door and the outhouse far enough away.

When they arrived Addie tied the pony to a post. She went to Jess and placed her hands on her hips. "Do you want to attempt to get out or was the trip out here enough to convince you that you should have stayed in bed?"

He cocked one eye at her. "You appear distraught."

Her answer was a frown. "Your vocabulary surprises me."

"Me too." He grinned. "I was wrasslin' with a steer who got the best of me at a rodeo and that's what one of the clowns said."

"What happened?" she asked.

"I decked him with one punch."

"The steer or the clown?"

He offered a genuine smile and she smiled back.

Lottie had been scouting the cabin. She came to the wagon. "I think it's salvageable but it will take a lot of work."

"I'll have plenty of time. Doc says it will be six weeks before I can get back to help with the farm," said Jess. "It might be exactly what I need to get stronger."

"Do you want us to help you out of the wagon?" asked Lottie.

"No, I've seen enough. Addie filled me in on the problems. I can start with caulking. If you

ladies don't mind, I need to get back to the house."
The perspiration was forming on his forehead once
again.

"The next time you had better listen to me,"
Addie reprimanded. "I knew this was too much for
you. You were just being stubborn."

Jess didn't respond.

Addie knew he was in pain although he did
his best to hide his discomfort. "I brought a pain
pill with me. Lottie there's a jug of water in the
corner."

Lottie brought the water from the corner
of the wagon and pulled out the cork in the top.
Addie put the pill in Jess's mouth and the women
held the unwieldy jug so he could wash down the
medicine.

Addie walked the pony back to the house
while Lottie went to find Caleb.

Addie was relieved to see him coming on
the run.

He managed to get his friend out of the
wagon. With Addie's help they were able to get him
into the house on his rubbery legs and into bed.

"Are you goin' to need me any longer?"
asked Caleb. "I sent Lottie on home and I've got to
finish up at the barn."

"Go ahead," she replied. "I knew he shouldn't
have gone in that wagon. Jess is stubborn."

Caleb smiled at her. "No more than the rest
of us. Thanks for takin' such good care of him."

When Caleb left, Addie checked Jess's
injured rib cage. It looked sound. She had been

afraid the jostling of the wagon would cause him harm. But, there was no blood seeping through and the taped area felt secure. She had no desire to go into the office and try to work. Instead, she went to the kitchen and prepared a soothing cup of tea.

CHAPTER 22

Two weeks after the accident Jess was at the cabin.

In the office, Alex was drinking a cup of coffee while reviewing financial papers with Addie. "It appears Jess is well enough to move back to his place with the hired men," he said.

"He doesn't care to live with them," responded Addie. "He's been working on the cabin. If he could get the floor boards in it would be suitable for him to live there, but he isn't up to that strenuous work yet. It's been nice to have his company. This big house can get lonesome."

"You have Ella," said Alex.

"It isn't the same. I feel comfortable with Jess here." She added, "He taught me how to play poker."

Alex looked directly at her. "Don't get too comfortable."

Addie stared back. "I'm not exactly sure what you mean by that remark."

He didn't answer. "What does he need to get the cabin in shape?"

"Boards in the floor need replacing, new hinges on the door, the fireplace needs cleaning, and a coat of paint on the roof."

"I'll send a man out from town to take care of it."

"No, Alex. I know Jess and he would feel obligated to you."

He peered over his cup of coffee. "You seem to have gotten to know him well."

"Well enough," she answered.

Alex finished his coffee. "I'm going out to find Caleb. Then I'll go by and ask Jess if he would object to the hired help getting the cabin livable. Maybe he won't feel obligated with them lending a hand."

Addie brightened. "I think he would accept that idea. We can make a party of it. Lottie, Ella and I will fix a picnic. I've read that Amish people get together and have a barn raising. We can have a cabin do-over."

He reached out his hand and helped her up from her chair. "If that will make you happy, I'm all for it."

Addie hadn't felt this joyous in a long time. "I'm going to run over and tell Lottie. When do you think we can do it?"

"Let me square it with Jess. I'm sure there are enough odds and ends in the barn that we could start on it tomorrow. I'll have a talk with Caleb, which means I should get Jess's permission first. "

"Hurry," said Addie. "I can't wait to tell Lottie."

Alex found Jess inside the cabin chinking the cracks in the walls. "Good morning, Jess. How are you coming along?"

"Slow. I'm trying to use my other arm a little more so I don't get stove up, but it's a trial."

Alex looked around. It was a large room. In one corner there was a sink with a hand pump. "Does that work?" asked Alex pointing to the pump.

"It does now. Caleb worked on it and oiled it up. Water tastes pure as a spring."

"What do you say if I get the hired help to work on replacing the floor boards and cleaning the fireplace? Seems to me you could move out here and fix up the rest as you get stronger."

Jess stopped his work and looked at his employer. "Time for me to move out of the house?"

"Only if you are up to it. It would be good for Addie to get her bed back. I can't think the divan in her sitting room is comfortable for sleeping."

Jess turned back to work. "Is that the only reason?" he asked. A silence fell between them before he continued, "I know you're right. That's why I've been doing as much as I can to get this place in shape. I refuse to go back and live with those two hired men of yours."

"Then we understand each other," said Alex. "The men can scout up what you need. I suggested this to Addie. She said if you were fine with having help, she wants to make a party of it. Cabin do-over she called it."

A pleasant smile appeared as Jess turned to look at Alex. "Addie is a special girl."

"She is that," agreed Alex. "I'll set things up. We will start tomorrow."

Caleb was leading a horse into its stable. "Mornin', Alex."

"Good morning. I've got a proposition to discuss with you."

Caleb took the bridle off the horse and closed the half-door to the enclosure to come to where his employer stood.

Alex told him of the plan for the cabin with which Caleb agreed. It would set him back a day, but Jess is a friend. And, it didn't seem wise to buck the boss.

"Lottie will be glad to hear this." A childish smile appeared. "Did Addie tell you we are expecting a baby in the spring?"

"She did."

Alex shook his hand. "Congratulations."

"Guess everyone knew but me."

Alex didn't respond. "Have the men round up what's needed. We'll get started around eight in the morning."

"I've been setting aside some supplies," Caleb informed. "I'll tell Lottie. She's goin' to be mighty happy."

Alex was satisfied. "I believe we are all settled. I'll go on up to the house to give Addie the news, and then I am going for a long ride on my horse."

Caleb nodded before stepping back into the stall.

Addie couldn't have been more pleased once she heard of the plans. She rushed to tell Ella and they left together to confer with Lottie.

Alex went back to the stable and saddled his horse. The week had been tiring. It seemed

157

that every time he thought he could begin to close down his law practice someone else needed his help. He knew Addie was getting unhappy with this arrangement because much decision making fell on her shoulders. She had once said she didn't want to get trapped. He didn't want her to feel that way.

Alex rode out to the far fields where he got off his horse and sat on a downed tree. He needed to think. He was taking a big chance on the cattle he was keeping over the winter, which meant extra feed. What if they didn't produce as he hoped? They had the horses, the pigs, the sheep and the chickens that needed to be fed. The government buyers had been out three times. They were full of promises to buy but had not produced any purchase order even though there was a world war going on.

Alex rose from the tree and walked, leading the horse. If he dared to close up his practice would he be able to make a go of the big estate before he sold to the government? He had six people employed who depended on him to make the right decisions.

Then there was Adelaide. She deserved more. She was a young girl who liked adventure, and he was sixteen years her senior. He had been careful to keep their relationship on a business level. He wasn't sure how much longer he could keep that up.

Alex lifted himself into the saddle and spurred the horse into a gallop.

CHAPTER 23

At noontime the next day, Addie, Lottie and Ella were taking their picnic offering to the cabin do-over. Addie had hitched up the horse to the low wagon. The back dropped down to form a ledge; the perfect place to hold the food they had prepared. The day was cloudy without the threat of rain. Ella had baked bread and a ham. She made egg salad and baked beans, Lottie added fried chicken and apple dumplings. Addie prepared a box containing: plates, silverware, mugs, a jug of cold water, flour sack drying towels, a bar of soap and blankets to sit on.

The men had been working for four hours and were ready to take a break. Addie drove the wagon to the site where Lottie and Ella began assembling the feast while Addie secured the horse to a tree. It wouldn't do to have the horse bolt and upset the planned outing.

Addie grabbed the soap and towels and went into the cabin where she found Caleb and Alex laying planks. The hired men were sooty, dirtier than usual, from cleaning the fireplace and Jess was scraping a window.

"Lunchtime, gentlemen," she announced. "But first you need to clean up before you touch the food. Here are the towels and soap."

The hired men looked at her with disdain. Washing with soap and water was not their favorite form of entertainment, one reason Jess refused to stay with them any longer.

Addie looked directly at Jess, who was wiping his brow. "You look peaked. You should not push yourself. After you wash up, go sit on the bench on the porch and I'll bring you a plate of food. The rest of you can fill your plates when you're ready."

Before any of them could answer she turned and left.

Caleb smiled at Alex. "I can see why you hired her to run the office."

Alex grinned. "I suspect we had better get spruced up for lunch before we lay another board."

Jess was at the pump wiping his hands on the flour sack. "I'm ready for some food."

Caleb stood up and stretched his long body. "You haven't overdone, have you?" he asked his friend.

"Let's just say I'll be glad to sit a spell," answered Jess on his way out the door to sit on the porch bench.

Addie had filled a plate with food and poured a mug of water for him. "You look tired. You ride back to the house with us when we leave. You should take a nap."

"Thanks," he said and took the plate of food she held. "I'll be right fine once I eat."

First Alex, then Caleb came to the wagon, filled their plates and went to sit on the porch step.

The hired men came out together, got their food and left to sit under a tree away from the others.

Lottie spread a blanket on the ground where she and Ella sat eating their lunch. Addie was fussing around reorganizing the food dishes in the wagon.

"Addie, come and sit," said Lottie. "You're almost making me feel guilty for not helping you."

"I'm coming," answered her friend. "I wanted to make it look more organized."

"Miss Addie, I can take care of that," announced Ella. She started to get up.

"Sit right back down," ordered Lottie. "If Miss Adelaide thinks she needs to fuss around, we'll sit here and watch how well she performs."

Addie stood back with hands on hips and waggled her head. "Now, Miss Lottie Bell, don't you think that looks more appetizing?"

A sly look appeared on Lottie's face. "Your skill at arranging fried chicken is without equal."

Addie filled her plate, poured a mug of water and came to where the women sat. She handed her water to Lottie before lowering herself onto the blanket. "Isn't this heavenly?" she asked to no one in particular.

"I think this is fun," said Ella.

Alex called from where he sat on the cabin step. "Lottie, this chicken is almost as good as the chicken you made when we went to Caleb's camp."

"That's because that was cooked in dry Colorado and this is in humid Virginia," she called back.

"What we're missin'," kidded Caleb, "is Momma Cat droppin' her kittens. That made the chicken taste even better."

All four of them laughed at their private Colorado memory.

"I think about Mrs. Tygert and Tilly Stiles. I wonder if they still have the cats. I should write a letter," said Addie.

Lottie joined in. "Tilly Stiles seemed to have a change of heart, but I'm not sure how far I'd trust her. I think she deliberately sent Mrs. Tygert's cat, Teddy, away. Maybe she'll do that with the kittens when they grow into cats."

"You may be right," agreed Addie. "What do you think, Alex? You met Tilly."

He answered, "Let's be charitable and believe she has mellowed. She needed a good man to help smooth out some of the wrinkles in her personality."

Lottie laughed. "I suggested that. She put on a show for you, Alex. Maybe you should go out and pay her a visit."

"Now, Lottie, you be careful how freely you talk," admonished Caleb.

Alex was not offended. "I've got my sights set higher than Miss Matilda Stiles," he replied.

These words caused Addie to perk up her ears. Did Alex have someone she didn't know about? He wasn't as open as he had been in Colorado. Also, he was careful that they weren't seen together and all interactions were on a businesslike level. The possibility that he had a romantic interest had not occurred to her until this moment. Suddenly, the day didn't seem as bright and cheerful.

After eating, the men prepared to go back to work.

"Jess, you are to return to the house with us," commanded Addie. "Dr. Hawthorne has told you to not overtax yourself."

"I'm going back in to finish."

Addie stood her ground. "No you're not. You get in this wagon. If you backslide, you'll be right back on the pain medicine and that isn't smart."

Alex came to her aid. "I believe Addie is right. We'll finish up this cabin in living condition so you can move in and be on your own. It wouldn't do to wear yourself out."

Jess understood the intent of his employer's statement. The quicker he was out of the house the better Alex would like it.

A half- smile appeared. "Guess you're right, boss." He climbed up on the seat of the wagon and waited.

The women cleaned up the remains of the picnic and loaded it into the wagon.

Caleb came to Lottie and kissed her on the cheek. "Thanks for the lunch, sweetheart."

She kissed him back. "You're welcome."

She and Ella got into the wagon bed. Addie unhitched the horse and took the driver's seat next to Jess.

Caleb and the hired men went back into the cabin but Alex stood and watched as the wagon pulled away with Addie and Jess shoulder to shoulder. It was definitely time for that good-looking cowboy to move out of the house.

CHAPTER 24

The next week Alex brought the mail from town. He tossed an envelope in front of Addie as she sat typing a letter. She stopped and looked at the postmark.

"It's from Clay!" she exclaimed.

"I noticed," replied Alex. "I'll take a walk so you can open it in private."

"Stay right here. There isn't anything he has to say that you are not to hear. Aren't you interested in where he is or what he's doing?" she questioned.

"Certainly, but the letter is not addressed to me."

"Don't be so righteous. He was probably pressed for time when he wrote."

Alex offered a crooked smile. "Probably."

Addie tore open the envelope, careful to keep the return address intact.

September 10, 1917

My dear Addie,

As I write this missive, my fellow soldiers and I are aboard a troop ship carrying us to Europe. We have had little training in warfare, but I understand we are to be trained by the French once we arrive wherever it is we are going.

The sailors tell us they are always on the lookout for German submarines that could blow us out of the water. I don't know if they are trying to scare us or if it is the truth. Every once in a while I find myself peering over the edge into the deep and wondering what may be lurking below.

In these few weeks I have learned the military does not explain. Those in charge give orders and we are to follow them without question. Don't misunderstand. I am not sorry to have joined up, but I am one who has been used to having things my way. The army has given me a sense of honor to do something for my country.

We have been on the ship four days. Many of the men have gotten seasick from the rolling of the waves. So far I have escaped. It is quite pleasant out here in the middle of the ocean with nothing but the sky over head and water all around.

The sailors do most of the work. That is not surprising because the ship is their home.

Many emotions run among the men in my outfit. Some of them have left families behind and some married within the week of sailing. To my way of thinking that was foolhardy on their part. What if they don't return? They will leave a widow after only one week of marriage.

I try to keep my thoughts on the sunny side but homesickness creeps in every once in a while. I like to think of you standing on the porch of Alex's grand house with the lovely Blue Ridge and rolling hills all around. Preferably that you are thinking of me.

I have decided to finish out my year at the university when I return. I may go to the School of Pharmacy. People will always need a druggist. Then I can look for a lovely place in Clarke. Think about it Addie, it is something we could both work for.

How is Alex? I wish I had gotten to know him better as a brother. He is someone I do look up to. I think about that now and wish I had expressed those thoughts to him before I left.

It is strange on the ocean how one's thoughts seem to tumble one upon the other. Good memories, bad memories, things you are happy you did and things you wish you had done all spill out one after the other.

I may not get a chance to write again for quite some time. I wanted you to know that I am well. Tell Lottie I send my regards. I hope all is well at Lockwood (I think Alex could have thought of something more original).

Please write to me at the return address. I understand the military is good at getting the mail through.

My most pleasant thoughts are of you.
Affectionately,
Clay

Addie held the letter before returning it to the envelope.

Alex looked at her, then spoke. "I thought you told him you were only interested in being a friend."

"I did."

167

He sat for a quiet moment. "I don't believe he took you seriously. You couldn't have been too forceful."

Addie smirked at him. "If you are inferring that I led him on, you can erase that idea from your mind." She pushed her chair away from the desk and stood. "What difference should it make to you? Looking out for your little brother? Hah!" She walked out of the room.

Alex sat there. He had not meant to upset her. He wished he had not stayed to listen to the letter. It did not set well with him that his brother still held a flame for Adelaide. Why did life have to be so complicated?

Alex left the house and went to the cabin Jess had moved into. He found Jess sitting on the porch whittling a whistle.

"How are you doing?" he asked.

"Feeling stronger. Caleb moved my cot in and brought a chair. The women set me up with some dishes. They think I need curtains at the windows."

"Do you?"

"I don't, but you know how women are. I expect one day I'll come in and they'll have fancied it up."

"I'll be happy to get whatever you need," said Alex.

"Thanks, but I'm fine. Addie insists that I take my meals at the house. She says I won't eat right if I'm by myself."

"Ella can bring them here," suggested Alex.

A teasing smile appeared. "It works out dandy. The walk to the house does me good."

Alex returned the suggestive smile. "I'm sure it does. I expect that in two weeks you will be able to assume most of your duties on the farm."

"Guess that's up to Doc Hawthorne," replied Jess and went back to the fine whittling of a whistle.

Alex turned and walked toward the stable. He felt the need for a fast gallop through the countryside.

Addie was so rattled by the words exchanged between her and Alex that she decided to pay a visit to Lottie. Lottie was home working on the Singer sewing machine Leopold Goldman had generously sent to her.

Lottie heard her knock and called, "Come on in, Addie. I saw you as you were coming down the path."

Addie came in and took a chair at the table where Lottie sat. "What are you making?"

"Curtains for Jess's cabin. It looks forlorn with only the cot and the overstuffed chair. He says it's comfortable enough for him."

Addie agreed. "Any man would say that. He needs a table with a couple of chairs at least. Where did you get the material?"

"Bits and pieces. I sewed them together to look like a patchwork quilt. Remember the shirt you had to cut off him when he got kicked?"

Addie nodded. "That was a mess."

"I brought it home, washed it up and salvaged what I could." Lottie stopped sewing and cut the thread. "What do you think?" she asked as she held up the short panel.

Addie looked it over. "It's handsome. He can't complain that it's too frilly. You've got to make three more of these. Do you have enough material?"

Lottie pointed to a pile on a chair. "I've made them. Patched curtains. I even made one for the front door. Caleb says he is going to get a door with a window in it because the cabin is too dark with only those two small windows."

"How did you know what size to make?"

"Caleb held up his hands and said it would be about so big." She held up her hands for Addie to see.

This brought a chuckle. "You are the one who is always so precise on measuring."

"There are times when it is all right to let things slide." Lottie rose from her chair. "I'm heating water for tea. I'm not sure what has brought you here but I have a feeling it will go better with a spot of tea."

"It's Alex. He can be so irritating."

"And you can't be?" Lottie said as she put the teakettle over.

Addie ignored her. "Clay sent a letter. He sends you his regards."

"Where is he?" asked her friend.

"Somewhere in the middle of the Atlantic Ocean on his way to France, he thinks."

"He thinks?"

Addie sighed. "Yes, he said the military doesn't tell them anything. They just give orders and expect the troops to follow them."

Lottie poured the tea into mugs and came to where Addie sat. "That doesn't sound like the Clayton Lockwood I know."

"He says he is happy. He is going back to the university after the war and may become a pharmacist."

Lottie took a sip of tea and looked at Addie. "Where do you fit in?"

"He said he wants to eventually buy a place here in Clarke and, listen to this, it is something we can both work for."

Lottie smiled. "Still carrying the torch."

"Alex was there when I read the letter and he all but accused me of leading Clay on."

"So you had to make some kind of reply that led you here."

Addie wrinkled her nose. "Don't be so wise. Yes, I did make an unkind remark."

Lottie sat for a moment. "The problem, as I see it, is that you care for Alex and he cares for you. He doesn't show it because he doesn't know how you feel and he can't afford to have word get around. Clay muddies the water because Alex doesn't want to trample his brother. You keep your guard up at all times so you don't get hurt."

171

A dejected Addie thought about Lottie's reply. "I know you're right."

"What are you going to do about it?"

Addie sipped her tea. "I've been thinking. First of all, I am going to the cinema with Jess. He asked me before the accident and he is well enough to go now. I need to get away from this place and he is fun to be around."

"Don't dig your hole any deeper," advised Lottie.

"Once I have repaid my obligation to Alex, I am leaving and finding a job in Washington."

Lottie was skeptical. "Is that really what you want?"

"At this moment it is," Addie answered. "Lottie, you are so fortunate. You know exactly what you want and it has fallen into place for you."

"Therein lies your problem, my friend. You don't know exactly what you want."

Addie thought about this. "You know. You are right. I will have Alex paid off by the end of October. The winter months will not be as demanding at the farm and it will be a perfect time to leave. I am going to contact Miss Stevens at the secretarial school and tell her that I will need a position by November. That will get me away, and Alex can handle the farm without it being a burden. Oh, Lottie, you have solved my difficulties."

Lottie smiled in her quiet way. "I believe you solved your own. Keep your eye on the prize, Addie, whatever that may be."

Addie stood up to leave. "Look at me. I came here and haven't even asked you how you are feeling. I couldn't help but notice that the little Dunn is beginning to show."

A wide grin creased Lottie's face. "He is and he is beginning to move about. I feel great."

Addie hugged her friend. "I am so happy for you. Let me know when you want to hang the curtains so I can help."

"Promise," answered Lottie.

Adelaide Mae Richards walked back to the big house with more of a spring in her step.

CHAPTER 25

Charlie Richards, on horseback, sped up the drive to Lockwood. He hopped from the saddle and knocked on the kitchen door, unprepared to see the pretty girl who answered his knock.

Charlie removed his hat and gulped before he was as able to speak. "I'm Adelaide's brother and I need to talk to her."

"Come in," invited Ella. "Miss Addie is in the office. I'll show you where."

Addie heard them coming down the hall and rose to see what the commotion was about. "Charlie!" She hugged her younger brother. "What brings you out here?"

Still clutching his hat, he said, "Aunt Lilly is at our house with CJ and he's awful sick."

"Why doesn't she take him to Dr. Hawthorne?"

Charlie turned his hat round and round. "He ain't in town. Momma and Aunt Lilly both want you to come."

She knew her mother would not send her brother to fetch her if it wasn't important. "Tell Momma I'll come as soon as I can get there."

Ella hadn't moved and Addie turned her attention to the young girl.

"I'll call Mr. Alex and tell him that I will be gone," Addie told her. "Go out to the barn and tell Caleb to hitch up the small buggy for me."

Ella ran from the house to do her bidding.

"Go on ahead, Charlie. Momma needs to know that I'm coming."

Charlie didn't have to be told again. He left the house, bolted up onto his horse and went racing for home.

Addie dialed the number to the law office.

"Alexander Lockwood's office," came the voice of the prim and proper secretary, Jane.

"This is Adelaide Richards. I need to talk to Mr. Lockwood."

"Mr. Lockwood is quite busy, Miss Richards. Is there a message I can give to him?"

Addie was vexed. No matter how many times she had called the office the protective Jane was cautious of letting her speak to Alex. "You may relay to him that I will be at my mother's house if he needs to contact me." She slammed the receiver back onto its hook.

Ella returned breathless. "Jess is hookin' up the horse. I couldn't find Caleb."

"Thank you." Addie was closing up her valise. "I'm not sure how long I will be gone."

"Do you want I should tell Miss Lottie?"

"That isn't necessary. If she comes by you may tell her I had to leave because my little cousin is sick."

Jess drove the buggy to the front porch and gingerly climbed from the driver's seat.

Addie hurried down the steps. "Thank you, Jess. I hope you didn't strain yourself getting this rig ready."

"I figured you really needed it in a hurry. Ella's eyes bugged out of her head like she'd seen a spook."

Addie couldn't help but smile. "Jess, be kind. She was upset. I am in a rush."

He helped her up onto the seat. "Not bad news, is it?"

"My young cousin is sick and my mother wants me to come home. I'm not sure what help I will be."

He kept his work-worn but gentle hand over hers. "Just having you there will bring a ray of sunshine. We still have a date for the cinema?"

She looked at him. "I didn't promise. But, I have a feeling that I will want something uplifting after I make this trip."

"That's good enough. Maybe we can talk Lottie and Caleb into going with us." Addie had not expected Jess to propose that possibility. Now that he had, the suggestion relieved any qualms about attending a picture show with this engaging cowboy.

Addie kept the horse at a swift pace until she reached her mother's house. Her brother, Chip, was waiting for her. "I'll take care of the horse and buggy, Addie. We're glad you came."

"Thanks, Chip. I'll grab my valise and then you can put it away."

Laura Richards heard her daughter's arrival and came out onto the porch. "Lilly's in a bad way," she said.

"Charlie said CJ is very sick."

"He is and Lilly is afraid she's going to lose him."

Addie hurried into the house where she found her aunt sitting in the rocking chair, cuddling her son, and staring off into space.

"Aunt Lilly," said Addie as she touched her aunt's shoulder.

Lilly looked at her. "Oh, Addie. I'm so glad you're here. My baby is so sick and the doctor isn't here."

Laura spoke up. "He won't be back until later this evening. CJ is burning up with fever and Lilly says he's been throwing up since yesterday. Weak as he is, he can't go on like this."

Addie cringed. She knew how concerned her mother was, but why did she have to use those words in front of Lilly?

Addie took her mother aside. "You've taken care of plenty of sick children. You know better than I what should be done."

"I wanted to sponge him down with cool water to get the fever out of him but Lilly said to wait until you came. She puts a lot of stock in you, Adelaide. Lilly thinks because you worked in a drug store you might know what's better to do. She's tired out with worry."

Adelaide was perplexed. She hadn't worked in a doctor's office, she had only helped in the

177

drug store. Taxing her brain for solutions she did remember one instance that might help.

"Once, the druggist told me that aspirin is best for fever and can be dissolved in water and given like an enema. It has to be given slowly so that it has a chance to absorb. Do you think Aunt Lilly will go along with that?"

This put a spark of life into Laura. "I've never heard of that but we have to do something. He's floppy as a rag doll. I've got that syringe with the long rubber tube that we feed the orphan sheep with. Do you think that would work?"

"Be sure and clean it up good," ordered Addie. "I'll see if I can get Aunt Lilly to understand what we want to do."

She returned to the rocker where her aunt had drifted back into her world of escape. She came to when Addie approached. Addie explained that they needed to get the fever down and how they were going to attempt it.

"I wish the doctor was here," said her aunt.

"So do I. He will come as soon as he gets back into town. Will you let me and Momma try?"

"I'm very tired, Addie."

Lilly looked so hopeless and helpless Addie fought back tears. "I know you are. Go in and lie down on Momma's bed and I'll hold CJ for you."

"Be careful with him. I trust you, Addie."

Laura Richards stood in the background. She came forward as Lilly transferred the limp child into Addie's arms. Laura took her sister's arm and led her into the bedroom.

"I should stay with him," apologized Lilly.

"No, you need some rest. You've been up all night. We'll come get you if we need to."

Those words relieved the exhausted mother and she closed her eyes as she lay her weary head on the pillow.

Addie went to Laura as soon as she closed the bedroom door. "Hurry, Momma."

Laura replied,"I've got everything ready on the table. We can lay him down there."

"Did you put an aspirin in the water?"

"I did. I only made half a cup."

"That will do. We should bathe him with cool water afterwards," advised Addie.

"I know," said her mother. "I'll do that while you see if the aspirin concoction is going to work. I can't see how Lilly let him get into such a state. She should have come in yesterday."

Addie lay the little three-year-old on the kitchen table.

"I wish Dr. Hawthorne hadn't told her that CJ may not live long. Although Aunt Lilly says that she and Uncle Frank are resolved, I don't think a mother can ever be resolved to that. Maybe CJ doesn't have a weak heart. Maybe it's something Dr. Hawthorne isn't familiar with."

"Children die, Adelaide."

"Let's say our prayers that it isn't going to happen to this little one. And we'll say an extra prayer that Dr. Hawthorne gets here sooner than expected."

The two women worked together. Whether they were going to be successful or not, they had to do what they thought was best.

After an hour, CJ wasn't any more responsive, but he didn't feel as hot as he had before they started.

"We should try to get some water into him," suggested Addie.

"Tea might be better," replied her mother. "Let's wait a bit."

Lilly came out of the bedroom and walked to where the women stood. "How is he?"

"He's not as hot," said Laura. "You didn't rest long."

"It was enough." She placed her hand on CJ's forehead and then kissed him. "He feels cooler."

"I'm going to fix some weak tea," said Laura. "Lilly you go sit in the rocker and you can spoon some into him."

Lilly took her child into her arms. "It may not stay down."

"It's worth the chance," said Adelaide.

Dr. Hawthorne arrived at four-thirty. He carried his bag from the Model T. Those in the house had heard the car rattle up the lane and opened the door before he could knock.

"We're all happy to see you," greeted Adelaide. She told him the story as he walked to where Lilly sat in the rocking chair.

"Been a rough time for you, Lilly," he said.

She burst into tears.

The physician took the child from her arms and laid him on the kitchen table. He took CJ's temperature and listened with his stethoscope. "He's dried out."

Addie told the doctor how they had handled the fever and he agreed they had done the right thing. He pulled a rubber bag of sterile water from his kit. Then he attached a long tube with a needle on the end.

"I'm going to give him some fluid before I take him to my office. The nurse can look after him there. He's still got a fever and his heart is pounding like a race horse."

Dr. Hawthorne cleaned the area on CJ's leg where he planned to insert the needle. He squeezed the muscle of the thigh and pushed the needle in where he secured it with tape. He tied the bag of water to an upper handle on a kitchen cabinet. "Laura you stand here and make sure he doesn't fall off the table while I talk to Lilly."

Adelaide walked out onto the front porch. She sat in the early October evening looking over the familiar space that had been her home. Her mind drifted to Clay and the fun times they had growing up. She wondered where he was at this moment and said a silent prayer that he would remain safe until this world war was over.

As she sat, her reverie was interrupted by the sound of a car engine as it came down the lane.

181

Alexander Lockwood exited the Franklin touring car and walked toward the porch where Addie sat. "Is everything all right? Jane told me you would be here."

He took a seat next to her on the bench.

"It's Aunt Lilly's little boy. Dr. Hawthorne is with them now. He is going to take him to the Hawthorne House where his nurse can watch him."

"You look worn out."

"I am," she admitted. "Momma sent Charlie up to the farm to get me. CJ looked so lifeless when I got here, I was as afraid he was going to die as his mother was."

"He's doing all right now?" he asked.

"He's in Dr. Hawthorne's hands, which is a relief to me. All I want to do is go back to the farm and crawl into my bed."

He smiled and took her hand in his. "I'll take you back in the car."

"I brought the horse and buggy. I should stay here overnight and drive it back in the morning."

"Ever the responsible Adelaide," he said. "You will ride back with me and I'll send one of the hired men for it tomorrow."

She should have held her tongue but the words slipped out. "Aren't you afraid Mrs. Talley will see us riding into town together and start a rumor?"

He wasn't offended. "Addie, when will you realize how things work? I will tell Jane. When Lavinia Talley drops by with the local news, Jane will set her straight as to how I acted like the Good Samaritan. I believe it is called covering the bases. You know Jane always stands up for me."

Addie offered a wry smile. "She's like a loyal dog. Whenever I call, she tries to find out if it is important enough to interrupt you, and I don't call unless it is necessary."

"She said you were abrupt with her over the phone."

"I hung up on her. I'm not sorry."

He stood and pulled her to her feet. "You had better go in and tell your folks you will be leaving."

"Come in and say hello. I know they heard you drive up."

She went into the house and Alex followed. "If you don't need me any longer, Alex will give me a ride back to the farm. He will send someone for the horse and buggy in the morning."

Dr. Hawthorne was closing up his bag. "Lilly. I'm unhooking this apparatus. You carry the boy and ride up to the Hawthorne House with me."

"Good to see you," he said as he noticed Alex had entered the room.

Lilly came over and hugged Addie. "Thank you, my sweet girl." Then she turned to Alex. "It has been many years and it is nice to see you again. You take care of our Addie."

Laura Richards stood near the stove. "It's about time for your pa and the boys to come in for their supper. You and Alex can stay for supper if you want."

Alex spoke up, "Thank you for the invitation, Laura, but Ella will have supper ready at the farm."

"Bye, Momma," said Addie.

Her mother was busy at the stove and didn't turn to look at her daughter. She said, "It was good you came, Adelaide."

What more was there to say? Addie turned and went out the door with Alex close behind.

She saw her pa and her brothers walking toward the house. Charlie was carrying Sarah Jane who had spent the day with Lottie's mother. Laura had instructed Chip to take her over to Mrs. Foster after Lilly's unexpected arrival.

Addie ran to her father. She threw her arms around his neck. "Pa, I haven't seen you for so long."

Her father held her close and patted her back as he had done when she was a little girl. "I've missed you, too. I know your momma was right happy to have you here."

Addie unwrapped her arms and wiped a tear from her eye. "I'm never sure with Momma," she said.

"Your momma holds her feelin's tight," he answered. "We're both proud of you, Things workin' out for you?"

"I think so."

The boys had gone on ahead and Alex was showing them his Franklin.

Addie took her father's hand as they walked to the car.

"How is your farm doin', Alex?"

"I'm pleased, John. I expect by spring I can shut down my lawyer's office. This war is a bad thing but it will be good for the farms. You should make a trip out and see these cattle I'm raising."

"I'd like to. I hear they are a special breed."

Alex grinned. "They are and come in all colors. The offspring will be full of surprises."

Addie had gone ahead and waited in the car.

Alex shook John's hand. "We'd better be on our way before the dark sets in. I'll send a man for the horse and buggy in the morning."

"They're safe for the night," replied Addie's father.

Dr. Hawthorne and Lilly, holding CJ, were settling into the Model T. "I'll follow you into town, Alex," he called.

Laura Richards watched from the kitchen window. She felt compassion for her younger sister as Lilly held her sickly child and stepped into the back seat of Dr. Hawthorne's car. Laura heaved a big sigh. She knew she should be thankful for her life, but that wasn't the way she felt. Trapped!

CHAPTER 26

Little Carroll Joseph, who had been a frail child all of his three years, was buried in Green Hill cemetery. Aunt Lilly considered Berryville her home because she was born and raised there. She had insisted on her child's final resting place and told Frank to buy a family plot "so we will all be together one day". Addie wondered if the sadness would ever go away.

The eleventh day of October was a pleasant Indian summer day. Friends and family gathered at the grave site before going to the funeral dinner, which was held at John and Laura's house. Frank Pierce, who was usually full of gruff and bluster, was devastated by the loss of his only son.

Alex had Ella prepare foods for the dinner for Addie and Lottie to take. He said he wanted to do something and Addie accepted.

Addie told Lottie she should stay at the farm because the strain of the funeral might be too much for her and her unborn baby.

Lottie wouldn't hear of it. "Your aunt was gracious to me and my mother and she will need help."

Other friends brought dishes to Laura's house. There was not enough room inside the tenant house so Laura had hired men to set up a long make-shift table near the house.

Addie and Lottie were taking care of the water, tea, lemonade, and coffee. Addie admired how well Aunt Lilly was handling the day. Perhaps the last few days at the Hawthorne House when CJ wasn't getting better had steeled her resolve. She'd had many months to get over the denial, anger, and guilt of CJ's frailty to finally accept that her baby would not be with her long.

Lilly came to her niece as she was putting a pot of hot coffee on the table. "Addie, I want to thank you for coming last week. With my little CJ at death's door, I felt I was losing my mind and having you there was solace for my soul. The summer you spent watching my girls showed me what a remarkable grown-up woman you have become. You have learned more in two years than I have learned in my thirty-two."

"Aunt Lilly, I can't tell you how sad and sorry I am about CJ."

"I know you are. Frank is taking it harder than I, but that is because he would never see the weakness. I have to be strong for my girls and for him. The scar will heal but it will never go away." Lilly hugged Addie tight. She whispered, "Don't be afraid to capture the happiness. Life is never a sure thing."

Addie watched her aunt walk away. Lilly greeted those who came and thanked them for their care and concern. As Addie watched from a distance, she realized that Lilly Pierce was a strong woman. It gave her an inward smile.

187

Lottie and Addie were both tired on the way back to Lockwood. Addie drove the buggy.

"I hope we never have to go through a day like that again," said Lottie.

"How do you feel? You were on your feet the whole time."

"They are beginning to talk to me." Lottie placed a blanket on the rim of the front of the buggy and put her feet up on it. "I'm glad I could be of help. There must have been a hundred people there."

"It just seemed that way. I believe Aunt Lilly was popular growing up and Uncle Frank comes from a large family."

Lottie looked over at her friend. "I overheard someone say that both your mother and your aunt were pretty girls."

Addie nodded. "I heard that about my mother, but I can't picture her being young and carefree."

"Do you think marriage and raising a family does that to a woman?" asked Lottie.

"Does what to a woman?"

"You know, makes them look old before their time and makes them carry worn and worried looks."

Addie chuckled. "You're a married woman and soon to have a family."

Lottie nodded. "I guess so, but I've never been pretty. Maybe it won't show so much on me."

"Gads, Lottie Bell. You come up with the strangest ideas. I think a woman's happiness might depend on the person she marries," mused Addie.

188

"Or, maybe it is the woman herself who decides to be happy or not."

Addie turned the horse up the road toward Lockwood.

"What makes you think that?" asked Lottie.

"I look at my mother. I don't think she's ever been happy and my pa is a wonderful man."

"You may be right. My mother seems satisfied with her life, even though my father likes his booze," replied Lottie. "Your mom, on the other hand, has never forgiven herself for getting married too soon."

Addie was on the lane leading to the farm and driving in direction of the barn.

"Why do you say that?"

Lottie took her feet off the blanket and tossed it into the back of the buggy. "The way she pushed you all the time. She was living her life through you, Addie. Couldn't you see that?"

"Maybe I didn't want to see it," answered Addie.

Lottie looked over at her and smiled. "If you didn't have a mind of your own, you would have gone to that normal school in Harrisonburg and ended up like Tilly Stiles, soured on life."

"Perish the thought," retorted Addie.

Jess came out of the barn. "Saw you two lovely ladies driving up the lane," he said. "You drive the buggy on in and I'll take care of putting the horse away. Did your day go all right?" he asked.

"Sad," they answered in unison. Addie and Lottie climbed down from their seats, with Jess's

189

help, and walked away. The experience of this day had given each of the young women much to think about.

CHAPTER 27

Addie hung up the phone on the receiver hook. Alex wasn't coming to the farm this weekend. He was going to James Anderson's place to look at a couple of horses. He also had an important legal case that would take him time to prepare so he would stay at his apartment in town.

It had been in the back of Addie's mind that Alex might have a girlfriend. Ever since the day of their cabin-do-over, when he jokingly said he had his sights set higher than Tilly Stiles, Addie wondered if there was someone she didn't know about.

James Anderson had found a woman with means and married her for her money. Why not Alex Lockwood? No, Addie reasoned that Alex was not that type. Or was he? He was concerned about the state of the farm. It would be a burden lifted if he knew he was financially set and could devote his time to what he truly wanted to do, which was to raise cattle and horses.

Addie pushed the ledger aside. It was Friday and the weekend would be long and lonely. Why not tell Jess she wanted to go to the cinema on Saturday? Yes, that was a good thought. First she would check with Lottie.

On her way out of the house, Addie saw Ella in the kitchen and told her that Mr. Lockwood would not be here this weekend. That information pleased Ella because she wanted to visit her family. She could go this evening and not have to be back until Monday morning if that was all right with Miss Addie. Adelaide agreed.

Lottie was sitting in front of the fireplace hand-sewing some baby clothes. She called, "Come in," when she heard Addie knock.

Addie took off her wool shawl. "Do you invite everyone in without knowing who it is?" she asked.

Lottie didn't move. "I knew it was you. You have a certain knock."

"I don't believe you," said Addie. "You didn't want to get out of that chair."

Lottie grinned. "I saw you coming down the lane."

Addie took a seat in the chair next to her friend. "How would you and Caleb like to go to the picture show tomorrow night?"

"Someone is getting antsy," observed Lottie. "I'll have to ask Caleb. What's playing?"

"I don't know. I just know that I need to get away. Alex is not coming out this weekend and Ella is going to visit her family. That big house gets lonesome, quiet and creepy at times."

Lottie smiled at her best friend. "You can stay in my extra room upstairs."

"I'm not afraid to stay by myself, but I'm ready to get out for something different."

"I'm sure Caleb will be all for it once he hears Alex won't be around to give him more to do."

Addie was enthused. "If you're sure, I'll see if Jess is in his cabin and tell him. He has asked me to go to the cinema three times."

Lottie sat her sewing aside. "Jess likes you, Addie. Don't let him think you care for him if you don't."

Addie was miffed. "You sound like Alex when I mentioned Clay. I will tell Jess that I agree to go to the cinema together as friends. Does that make you happy?"

Lottie thought about it. "It isn't any of my business. You and Jess are both grown-up enough to know your own minds. At least I think you are."

"Do you want to go or not?" asked a perturbed Adelaide.

A teasing smile appeared on Lottie's wholesome chubby face. "I wouldn't miss it," she answered.

"Good. It's settled. I'll find Jess and tell him." Addie gave Lottie a hug before she hurried out the door.

Jess was cleaning up branches behind his cabin as Addie came around the side. "Hi Jess," she called.

He stood up with a bundle of dry sticks in his arms. "This is a surprise," he said. "I hope it isn't bad news."

"No it isn't. How would you like to go to the picture show tomorrow night with Lottie, Caleb and me?"

He dumped the load of sticks into a pile and looked over at her. "What's the reason?"

"Because you've asked me to go and I never gave you a sure answer."

Jess pushed some dirt around with his boot. "The boss not coming out?"

"What makes you ask that?" she questioned.

"Because, when he comes you stick close to the house. He might not like the idea of you going out with me."

"Jess, I am not going on a date with you. We will go as friends. Alex isn't going to care if we are seen at the cinema together. It won't harm his reputation in the community," she informed.

He came to where she stood. "I don't think it's his reputation he would be worried about."

Addie was annoyed. "Jess, you don't make sense. Lottie, Caleb and I are going to see a moving picture tomorrow night and if you want to come, you can."

He took her hand and kissed her fingers. "Miss Adelaide, I would be most happy to accompany you to the cinema…as a friend." He turned his ruddy handsome face up and winked.

She snatched her hand away but couldn't hide the fluster she felt. "Why don't you have an accent like Caleb? You're both from Oklahoma."

"Different backgrounds," he answered, without further explanation. "What time are we to leave?"

"I told Lottie six o'clock."

"Do you want to come inside and see what I've done with the one room?"

"No thank you. I saw it when Lottie and I hung the curtains. There is only so much you can do with one room and a dearth of furniture," she said.

He did his best to entice her. "I've hung a picture."

"I'll see it another time."

"I redid an old table and a couple of chairs. Sure you don't want to see them?" he persisted.

"All right," Addie answered. "If that's what you want, I'll go in and look."

A used door with a large window had been found for the cabin. Jess had sanded and varnished the relic giving the door a fine sheen. He held it open for Addie to enter.

Over the mantle hung a portrait of a well-groomed family, which caught her eye the minute she stepped into the room. The wide heavy frame was wood with metal embellishment around the edges. "What a lovely picture," she exclaimed.

"That's my family," said Jess.

Addie walked to the fireplace to get a better look at the picture that hung above it. "Where was this taken? You must be the little one sitting in front."

He pointed. "Yes, that's me. My mother and father and four sisters."

195

"Coming from Oklahoma, I thought you might be part Indian."

Jess laughed. "Maybe Iroquois."

Addie smiled. "You didn't say where you came from."

A look of nostalgia crossed his face. "Central New York area. I was the restless type. As soon as I finished school, which my father insisted on, I left the area looking for adventure."

"Did you find it?"

He sighed. "Found I liked ranching and didn't like panning for gold. Want some tea?"

"I should be going." When Addie turned she saw the table and chairs he had refinished. "Jess!" she cried as she ran to touch them. "How beautiful. I didn't know you could do this kind of work." She ran her hand over the smoothness of the table.

He came up beside her. "There's a lot you don't know about me, Addie."

Uncomfortable with his nearness, she walked to the door.

Jess didn't move but there was laughter in his eyes.

"I'll see you tomorrow evening," she said and left. Addie took a deep breath of the cool air. What was it about Jess that stirred inner feelings? Perhaps it was because she had been his caretaker when he was injured. Whatever the cause, she didn't care for the feeling.

**

196

Addie dressed in the green suit Lottie had made for her. She sat in the rocking chair on the front porch listening for the buggy. The late October air was already cool. She wore a warm shawl, brown leather gloves and her brown straw hat. A blanket rested on the chair next to her and would be her cover if the night became too cold. The sun was almost down. Addie could see the shadow of the Blue Ridge. The splendor of fall colors had been glorious during the day but now the trees looked ominous in the dimming light. Her thoughts turned to Clay and she upbraided herself for not having written to him. She would do that tomorrow.

The buggy was coming up the lane. Caleb had tied sleigh bells on it because he didn't want a car to run into them on the main road. Addie thought that foolish. There were few people who owned automobiles. It could prove embarrassing to ride into town with bells announcing their arrival.

Jess hopped out of the backseat and met Addie as she was coming down the stairs. He took the blanket from her arm and helped her up into the back of the buggy before he took a seat beside her. That was unexpected. Lottie was supposed to ride next to her, or so Addie had planned.

Lottie turned her head toward the back seat. "Hi, Addie. Do you know what's playing? You didn't tell me the other day."

"I don't know. I guess I should have asked Alex to check."

"As long as it isn't some depressing war movie like we saw the last time," Lottie said.

Jess suggested. "Maybe we'll get the Keystone Kops. I can do with some laughs."

Caleb turned the horse onto the main road to ride the five miles to town. "We can all do with time away from the farm," he surmised.

"Lottie, I'm going to write a letter to Clay tomorrow. Do you want to put a note in it?" asked Addie.

"You can tell him that I hope he is safe and I keep him in my prayers."

"Who is Clay?" asked Jess.

Addie faced him. "He's Alex's younger brother. He and I grew up together on the farm where we lived until his parents sent him to boarding school."

"Where is he?"

"In the cavalry. He sent a letter a couple of weeks ago that he was on a ship headed to France. I don't know much about this war," said Addie.

"You're concerned," observed Jess.

"Of course I am. Clay is like a brother to me," she blurted out.

Lottie turned her head to look at Addie. "Are you sure he isn't more than that?"

Lottie didn't need to say that, thought Addie. Maybe it was to warn Jess. Whatever the reason it could have been left unsaid.

"It's goin' to be a right pretty night," said Caleb. "The dreary and wet November is around the corner. We'll have to be keepin' those cows close to the barn in the winter months, Jess."

Addie was pleased to have a new subject of conversation. She and Jess were sitting with hips touching and the buggy wasn't big enough for her to move apart.

"Lots of feeding and cleaning ahead," replied Jess. "I hope those two hired men stick around. What if I get called into the war or decide to head back to Oklahoma?"

"They aren't likely to call us off the farm and that little cabin will keep you warm and snug in the winter. I don't think the movin' bug will hit you until spring," said Caleb.

Jess laughed. "You're right." He turned to Addie. "Looks like you're stuck with me for a few more months."

Caleb unhooked the sleigh bells before coming into town. They rode past Alex's law office where Addie noticed a dim light was on. Could it be that Alex did have a pressing legal case? The sight gave her a warm feeling. Then an idea popped into her mind. Wouldn't it be a nice surprise to fix his dinner and bring it to him tomorrow?

Caleb parked the buggy on Church Street and the four passengers walked to the opera house where the cinema was located in the back. They were early enough to get seats in the second row to watch a Charlie Chaplin film.

At intermission Addie and Lottie both spotted Nettie, the clerk from Coyner's, and her husband, George. Addie introduced them to Jess. Nettie's eyebrows flew up. What a nice little item to tell Lavinia Talley, Adelaide Richards being seen out with one of the hired men at Lockwood. And, Lottie Bell expecting a baby in the spring was almost more news than Nettie could bear. She twittered away with mundane conversation ending with, "It is so good to see you both again." George stood at his wife's side the whole time without saying a word, although he had nodded his head. After they walked away Addie whispered in Lottie's ear, "I think rumors will be flying."

The moon was shining after the film was over. Caleb hooked up the bells because they could possibly meet a car and he didn't want to take the chance of an accident. Addie and Lottie both bundled up in the blankets they brought but Caleb and Jess braved the cool of the evening with their jackets.

As they had done before, the men serenaded the women with western songs they knew and told funny stories about their work on ranches. By the time they reached the farm all four were in a jovial mood.

"I'll see you in," said Jess.

"That isn't necessary," said Addie.

"I'll see you in," he repeated. "Go on ahead Caleb and take Lottie home. I'll come help you unhitch the buggy."

"I'll take care of it," replied Caleb. "Night Addie, night Jess."

"Bye, Addie," called Lottie as the buggy pulled away. "Don't forget to write Clay that I wish him well."

Jess walked Addie up the steps. She unlocked the door. "I'm fine Jess."

"I'll see you inside and check that everything is all right."

"What could be wrong?" said Addie.

"Are you sure you don't mind being here by yourself?"

"Jess, I'm fine."

The moon cast low light in the room and Addie turned to go into the parlor to light a lamp when a rustling sound like someone rummaging around reached their ears. Addie's eyes opened wide as she looked at Jess. "What's that!" she whispered.

"Coming from the kitchen," he whispered back. "Stay here."

Addie waited. As soon as Jess entered the kitchen, she heard scuffling, then a thud and then she heard Jess. "God almighty! I'm sorry, Alex."

Addie ran into the shadowy kitchen and turned on the kitchen light. Alex lay on the floor like a stone".

"I thought he was an intruder," Jess apologized.

Addie ran to where Alex lay flat as a pancake. She tapped his cheeks. "Wake up, wake up!"

Jess brought over a cold wet rag. "I think he's going to be okay. I didn't hit him too hard. I don't think I did."

"Jess you're a head taller and probably fifty pounds heavier. You might not know your own strength."

Jess was put out with her. "I haven't been at full strength since that bull almost did me in. He'll be all right."

After the wet rag roused him, Alex opened his eyes before raising his hand to his face, which was beginning to swell.

"I was hungry," he said.

Addie still knelt by his side. "Alex, you said you weren't coming this weekend."

He sat up with Jess's help. "I got that legal case resolved and decided to come."

Alex eyed Jess dressed in a white shirt, string tie and polished boots. Then he looked at Addie in her attractive green suit and her hair neatly coifed. "Where have you two been?" he asked.

"We took in the picture show in town," answered Jess.

"Just the two of you?" asked Alex.

"With Caleb and Lottie," Addie hurried to say.

Was that a relieved or questioning look in his brown eyes?

Jess helped Alex to his feet. "I think you're going to have a puffed up face and black eye for a while."

Alex gave a sarcastic reply, "That's sure to impress them in the courtroom."

"I sure am sorry," Jess repeated. "If you think you're all right, I'll be on my way."

Alex stood holding the cold rag to his face. "It's my fault," he admitted. "I'm glad you were here," he told Jess. "If it wasn't me, Addie could have been in trouble."

Addie walked Jess to the door. "Thank you for the cinema," she said. "It was an interesting evening."

Jess took her hand. "Good night, Addie. The pleasure was mine. Take as good care of the boss man as you did for me." He kissed the fingers of the hand he held and let his eyes rest on her for a long minute before he turned in the direction of his cabin.

Addie saw the Franklin parked behind the house. She went back into the kitchen where Alex stood. "Are you still hungry?"

"I seem to have lost my appetite," he said. The puffiness of his face caused a crooked smile. "Good night, Adelaide. I'm going up to bed."

"Good night, Alex. Are you sure you're going to be all right?"

He nodded.

CHAPTER 28

Addie was up early the next morning. Because Ella wasn't there, she started a fire in the wood stove. She put coffee and water in the enamel coffee pot and set it on the stove burner to perk. The watch pin Clay had given her said nine o'clock.

When the stove was hot enough, Addie put an iron spider on another burner and melted bacon grease in it. Then she mixed a batch of pancake batter and whisked eggs together to make scrambled eggs. Alex would be hungry this morning. If he was late rising, she would keep the food heated in the oven, which sat on the right side of the stove.

The heat from the wood stove was warming up the kitchen. Although there was a fireplace in every room of the house they were always too hot next to them or too cold at the fringes. Addie put a couple of plates, two mugs and a small pitcher of maple syrup in the oven to warm. Putting hot food on cold plates cooled the food. Addie liked hot coffee, warm pancakes and eggs.

Addie wore an oversized, well-worn, navy wool cardigan with her navy wool skirt and brown, laced shoes. Her hair that had looked so perfect the night before was rumpled from tossing and turning during the night. She hadn't slept well. Perhaps it was the night out at the cinema, more likely it was due to the unexpected discovery of Alex and the blow he took from Jess.

Addie didn't have to wait to see how Alex was faring because he appeared in the doorway.

"I smelled coffee and I can use a cup," he said.

Addie had her back to the door and jumped when she heard his voice. She turned and could not suppress the laugh that escaped. "Alex, you're a mess!"

"This is nothing to laugh about, Adelaide."

"I know. I couldn't help it. Your face looks like Jess's side after he was kicked by the bull."

Alex sat in a chair at the kitchen table. "I didn't hear you laugh at him," he said.

Addie brought him a mug of hot coffee. "This will make you feel better."

Alex sipped the coffee with some discomfort due to his swollen lip.

"Don't you see any humor in it, Alex? You come home to your own house and unsuspectedly get smacked as an intruder."

"I find nothing humorous about it. I think I hit the back of my head on something when I went down."

Addie felt the back of his head under the short brown hair. "You do have a small goose-egg. Does your head hurt?"

"Everything hurts," he answered. "I have to appear in court on Monday. What am I going to tell people?"

His usual pleasant angular face was round as a melon.

"Tell them the truth because they will find out one way or another. We'll use witch hazel on it today and maybe some of the swelling will go down. The bruising will be there for a couple of weeks. Are you ready for pancakes and eggs?"

Alex sighed. "I can handle them. Good thing you didn't cook up any meat. My teeth hurt. I don't think I can chew."

Addie smiled. "You aren't going to do anything for the rest of the day. There will be no checking the cattle or the horses or looking around for what has to be done. If you don't have anything to read, I have Zane Grey books. You can read about the West."

"I've been there, remember? You wouldn't be here today if it wasn't for that worried call about Mrs. Tygert when you went to Colorado."

Addie took a chair opposite him. The recollection was vivid in her mind. "I often wonder if I would have come back here if it wasn't for you," she said.

He swallowed some pancake before saying, "Sure you would have. Lottie was coming back. You would have been by yourself."

She nodded her head. "I thought about that. I liked working at the drug store, but I did miss the eastern scenery."

"There are times when we would all like to get away to sort out our thoughts. I've found I can do that right here. This place is big enough that I can ride out to a far field and let my mind wander," said Alex.

"What thoughts do you have to sort out?" asked Addie. "Seems to me you're quite well set."

He gave a half-way grin. "You would be surprised."

After they finished their breakfasts, Addie got the witch hazel and dabbed it on Alex's swollen face. She had never been this close to him since he had comforted her when she was exhausted from caring for Jess. At that time it had been solace that she needed. Now, Alex needed her. In silence she began nursing his injury and wasn't prepared for the excitement she felt when she touched his face or when their bodies accidently brushed.

If Alex experienced any kind of a spark, he didn't let on.

She had tingled at the touch of Clay and of Jess, but Alex's touch was like a magnet pulling her close. She knew she would have to keep her distance.

"Apply the witch hazel every three or four hours today," she instructed. "I'm hoping your face will be back to semi-normal tomorrow, except for the bruising."

He pushed his chair away from the table. "Guess you'd better lend me one of those Zane Grey books you're so fond of. I don't feel like doing anything except sitting in an easy chair. When will Ella be coming back?"

"Tomorrow morning. I'll bake some custard and have mashed potatoes with gravy for supper."

"You shouldn't have to cook, Adelaide. That isn't why I hired you."

"Forget that I am an employee of yours and let me be a friend. At least for today."

Alex started to say something but changed his mind and walked from the room.

Addie cleaned up the soiled dishes. She found him sitting in the parlor. "Here's the book, The Lone Star Ranger. Have you read it?"

"I don't get much chance to read," he said. "This will be a luxury. Thanks for taking care of me, Addie."

If he only knew how much she cared for him. She handed him the book and said, "I'm going over to visit Lottie."

"Send Caleb up to give me an update on what's been going on."

She bowed slightly. "As you wish."

He apologized, "Sorry, I didn't mean it to sound like an order."

Addie turned to leave.

Alex called to her, "By the way, prepare him for my transformation. I don't want to hear a loud guffaw."

She smiled and nodded. "I can't promise he isn't going to break out in hilarity, but I promise that I will tell him of your condition."

When Addie reached Lottie's, Caleb was leaving. "Wait," said Addie. "Alex wants you to go up to the house and tell him what's gone on this week."

"Why doesn't he come out to the barn like he always does?"

Addie grinned. "When we got home last night, Alex was rummaging around in the kitchen with only the light of the moon shining in. Jess went in and before he knew who it was he popped him a solid punch. Alex now sports black eyes and a swollen face. You are not to laugh when you see him."

"I recall that time I got punched in the face when we were in Evergreen Cemetery," drawled Caleb. "No laughing matter."

"I know, but I couldn't help myself when I saw him this morning. He is always so well-groomed. I just wanted you to be prepared."

Caleb threw on his tall cowboy hat and left.

"Sit and have a cup of tea," said Lottie. "Something has brought you here this morning besides the crowning of the King of Lockwood."

Addie sat at the table. "You know me too well. I've got things on my mind."

Lottie poured tea for each of them. "Let me guess. Those things would be Clay, Jess or Alex."

"Mostly Alex," replied Addie. "I don't know how much longer I can work for him."

"What brought this on?" asked her friend.

"You know I care a lot for him. When I agreed to be his bookkeeper I thought it would be wonderful to work next to him."

Lottie sipped her tea. "It's not so wonderful?"

"I thought maybe he had some feelings for me, now I don't think so. I like what I do here, but I have been thinking about contacting Miss Stevens at the secretarial school to see what kind of a position I could get in the city."

"All because you don't think Alex is interested?"

Addie sat her cup down and hesitated. "Not completely. I think I need a change. When CJ died, Aunt Lilly told me to capture the happiness because we never know what to expect in life."

"Your leaving will put Alex in a bind," said Lottie.

"I have given this thought. The winter months are going to be slow so Alex can take care of the bookwork. Maybe he will finally give up his law practice as he should have done a couple of months ago."

"Is that what is eating at you? Because he didn't give up his law practice like you thought he should? That sounds selfish on your part, Addie."

"I don't think it is selfish. He told me that was what he planned to do."

Lottie countered, "He didn't say when. You know he wants to get this place on solid footing."

Addie became ruffled. "You're sticking up for him. His finances were in good shape before he bought that expensive bull that almost did Jess in. Then he bought those crazy-looking cows that he thinks are going to fetch a pretty penny with their offspring. What if they don't? Where will Alex Lockwood be then?"

Lottie didn't speak right away. She looked at her best friend. "Addie, maybe the best thing for you to do is to go away for a while. Get a job in the city and see if that is what you want. Alex won't look for anyone until the spring. You'll know by then whether you want to stay in the city or come back here."

Addie uttered a relieved sigh. "Oh, Lottie, do you really think that is what I should do? What if I hate it and Alex hires someone else?"

"That's a chance you will have to take. I would rather you didn't, but I've never seen you in such a turmoil. This isn't like you."

Addie wagged her head. "I know. I don't feel like me."

Lottie smiled. "Talk it over with Alex. See if he is willing to go along with the plan. Tell him you will let him know by the end of February if he has to start searching for a new bookkeeper. That sounds fair."

"It is scary to think about but I know I have to change something. I feel bad for what happened last night. It wasn't Jess's fault."

"Jess didn't hurt himself, did he?" asked Lottie.

Addie came to attention. "I didn't think to ask him. How thoughtless of me."

Lottie was practical. "He wouldn't tell you if he did."

"Do you think I should go over to the cabin and check on Jess?"

"No," answered Lottie. "I'll send Caleb to check on him when he gets back."

Addie lamented, "Alex looks so forlorn, I don't want to put another burden on his shoulders."

"He's a grown man, Addie. Grown men are supposed to handle adversity."

"But not all at once," answered Addie. "I'll bite the bullet and tell him what I am planning to do."

"Good," said Lottie. "Have you written to Clay, yet?"

"No, I haven't had time. I'll do that this afternoon. I'm going for a walk before I go back to the house," Addie decided.

"I'm going to bake a chicken," said Lottie.

Addie smiled. "I promised Alex baked custard and mashed potatoes. His teeth hurt from Jess's punch."

"Are you sure Jess didn't know it was Alex?"

"Lottie!" Addie exclaimed. "What a thing to suggest."

"Shame on me," said Lottie. "You'd better watch the sky because it looks like it's going to rain."

Addie hugged her friend. "Maybe a good soaking is what I need. Bye, Lottie."

Lottie watched Addie walk away. It will only take time, my dear Adelaide, thought Lottie.

CHAPTER 29

Ella returned early Monday morning and found Addie in the office. "Mr. Alex's car is parked out back," she said.

"Yes, I know," replied Addie. "He has to be in court this afternoon. He will be leaving soon and he can do with a good breakfast before he leaves."

"He ain't mad 'cause I wasn't here, is he?"

"No, he isn't. He came home unexpectedly and there was an accident here Saturday evening. I tell you this because he has a badly bruised face and I don't want you to be surprised."

Ella's eyes opened wide. "What happened?"

Addie knew she had to tell the truth and the story came out.

"That's awful," said Ella. "Jess is a lot bigger. Mr. Alex is goin' to be all right?"

"He will. I think it bruised his pride as well as his face."

Ella looked puzzled. "What do you mean by that?"

"Nothing worth explaining," replied Addie. "You had better get breakfast started. I expect he will be down soon."

When Alex appeared in the doorway of the office, Addie was pleased to see that the swelling in his face was lessened. He looked more like the Alex she knew. There was evidence of a small cut on his lip and both eyes were bruised, but he was dressed in a white shirt, plaid tie, and a three piece gray wool suit, every inch of him a gentleman, if you looked from the neck down.

"How do you feel?" she asked.

"Almost back to normal. I wouldn't appear in town today if it wasn't for that court case," he answered.

"Is there any way you can postpone it?"

"No," he said. "I want to get the blasted thing over. The judge wouldn't grant a postponement at this late date, anyway."

"Probably not," Addie agreed. "Ella is back and has your breakfast ready. You'll need substance to get through the day. You hardly ate anything yesterday."

"Come and have breakfast with me," he invited.

Addie rose from her chair and went to the dining room with him, where he pulled a chair for her to sit. "Your visit to Lottie's was longer than I expected. How is she?" he asked.

"Fine," she replied, without adding that she took a long walk before returning to the big house.

Ella brought their plates of food and coffee and returned to the kitchen. She must have taken note of her employer's bruised face, but she didn't let out a loud gasp as Addie had expected.

"Do you think she noticed?" Alex wondered.

Addie looked over and smiled. "I warned her ahead of time."

She wanted to tell Alex of her plan to contact Miss Stevens at the secretarial school but hesitated. This wasn't the time to tell him what she was planning. There would be another time for that.

They had a good breakfast and Alex told her the information Caleb had given him yesterday. Alex seemed quite pleased with the way the farm was headed. There was no need to send him off with questions in his mind. Addie listened, feigning interest.

She waved to him when he drove away in the Franklin. There were a couple of quick items to finish up in the office then she would write to Clay, which she had planned to do yesterday but the walk took longer than she allowed.

In the office, Addie typed a bill of sale for the pigs the government wanted to buy. All she would have to do is add the date and have the driver sign when he arrived. She knew she would hear the squeal and grunting of the pigs when they were rounded up. How she hated that noise!

It would be easy to type the letter to Clay, but good manners were to have it handwritten making it more personal. Addie pulled stationery from the drawer with the Lockwood emblem embossed in gold on the top.

October 20, 1917

Dear Clay,

I must begin with an apology that I haven't written sooner. I have no excuse except that I let time get away from me.

215

I think about you often and wonder where you are and how you are doing.

Before I forget, Lottie sends her well wishes to you. She and Caleb are expecting a baby in the spring. I wish you had taken the time to see Lottie and meet Caleb the day you stopped by. He seems perfect for her and she is contented with the life she has chosen. I wish that I could say the same for myself. I am still searching.

The good news is that the farm is doing well. The government has started to purchase goods from Alex because of the war. In fact, someone is coming to buy a load of pigs today. He has sold horses and mules also. The mules were some he and James Anderson bought over in West Virginia and resold to the government at a better price. You may not know James. He is from the southern end of the county and a top horse breeder in the area, which he is not shy about letting others know.

There is also sad news. I'm sure you remember seeing little CJ, Aunt Lilly and Uncle Frank Pierce's boy. Aunt Lilly was feeding him that day you came to Boyce while I was taking care of my cousins. Carroll Joseph was never a healthy child. A few weeks ago he became ill and was unable to recover even with Dr. Hawthorne's capable doctoring. CJ was buried in a family plot in Green Hill cemetery. The funeral reception was held at my parents' house.

Although the occasion was sad, the day was beautiful and it brought back memories of the good times we had growing up there on that big farm your parents own. I believe we knew every corner of that place and didn't leave a stone unturned. Perhaps one day it will be yours.

Soon it will be the first of November. That is not my favorite month because it is usually cold, wet and dreary. The business of the farm will lessen as winter sets in and everything seems to go to sleep until spring arrives with promise.

Alex has bought a breed of cows that he feels are going to be popular as meat producers in the coming years. He also bought a huge bull and is looking forward to the offspring of these cattle. They are a mixture of colors and their breed is from somewhere in the British Isles.

The bull is dangerous. He kicked one of the hired men and fractured his ribs. Jess is a friend of Caleb and skilled in the handling of cattle from working on ranches. It was a freak accident and, although Jess is a big and rugged cowhand, it has taken time for him to recover.

Oh yes, and you will get a kick out of this. Alex was not supposed to come to the farm over the weekend. I had gone to the picture show with Lottie, Caleb and Jess. When we arrived home we thought Alex was an intruder. Jess let fly with his fist before he realized who Alex was and Alex now sports two black eyes. He had a court case today. What kinds of tales do you think Lavinia Talley will spread around? Alex is not going to dodge her scrutiny.

Please write and tell me where you are and what you are doing. We don't get up-to-date news about the war. Alex brings home the Courier

217

*every week, which is old news once I get to read it.
I think we should subscribe to the Washington Post
newspaper but Alex says the news in the Courier is
good enough.*

*I don't know much about this world war we
are engaged in, but I pray it will be over soon so
you can return home.*

*All of us send our good wishes to you and
keep you in our prayers.*

*Your forever friend,
Addie*

She put the three-cent stamp on first, then
wrote the address Clay had written on the envelope
he sent. She placed the letter inside, dabbed her
finger in a jar of paste, ran it over the fold of the
envelope and sealed it. Whoever was going into
town could mail it in the post office.

Next she was going to call the long distance
operator to get the phone number at the secretarial
school. Lunch was from noon to one o'clock at the
school and the best time for Miss Stevens to come
to the phone without disturbing class. This is what
she wanted to do but it was unnerving to actually
make the call.

Addie held her breath when she heard
the operator say, "Long distance call from Miss
Adelaide Richards to a Miss Stevens." Addie didn't
know the woman's first name.

Miss Stevens must have been in the director's
office because she came to the phone right away.
"Lillian Stevens," Addie heard her say.

"Go ahead," came the operator's voice.

"Miss Stevens…"

"Adelaide, how nice to hear from you."

"I wasn't sure you would remember me," said Addie.

"I rarely forget one of our star pupils," she replied.

"Miss Stevens, I have been thinking about working in the city. When I left school, you said you had contacts and I am interested."

"I am so pleased to hear from you," she said. "The government has openings they need to fill because of the war. New positions seem to be opening up every day. The pay is good and I can help find a rooming house if that is necessary."

"I would need one," said Addie. She hadn't given thought to a rooming house.

"Give me your address and I will send you information about positions available, cost of room and board, and when you are available to interview."

Addie gave her the address, thanked her for her time and told her she would call her back as soon as she had made a decision. When she hung up the phone Addie realized she hadn't thought through the changes she would make if she left the security of the farm. Added expenses of a room, food, clothing, and transportation were enough to give her pause.

Then the thought came that she had to break the news to Alex. Once a decision was made it would remain her secret until the right time came to tell Alex and Lottie.

Addie startled when Ella appeared in the doorway.

Addie's head jerked up. "You were so quiet, I didn't know you were there."

"I came to ask if we were goin' to work on readin' or numbers tonight."

Addie had been spending one hour each evening, when she could, to teach the young girl.

"Numbers seem to be the most difficult for you so I guess that will be the choice."

"That's good. I took that "Peter Cottontail" story home with me and read it to my folks. They were right proud of what I learned and they thought it was a good story."

"I'm pleased you did," encouraged Addie.

"I wish you could have heard my pa laugh," said Ella. "Pa said it would teach that little bugger to listen to his ma."

Addie's wide smile went from ear to ear.

At the funeral dinner, her brother, Charlie, had asked about Ella. "She seems pretty nice and she's pretty too," he had said. Addie agreed with him. He also asked if he could ask her to go to the picture show. Addie thought that was a splendid idea. Charlie was a good person. He never liked school but he was a hard worker. Ella was a good student so if Addie could get her up to a sixth grade level, she and Charlie would be on equal footing and a good match. It was something to think about.

Addie heard the grunting and squealing of the pigs that were going to market. How had she missed the rumbling and rattle of the cattle truck?

It was important to get the sale paper signed and she didn't want to take the chance of the driver running off without signing so she filled the barrel of the ink pen with ink, blotted the nib on the blotter on the desk and hoped the fountain pen wouldn't leak.

She clipped the paper to a clipboard, grabbed her shawl and headed in the direction of the squealing pigs. The two hired men in charge of the pigs closed up the tailgate of the truck as she approached.

"You need to sign this," she said to the driver.

"For what? I don't sign papers."

His words did not set well with Addie.

"You have to sign this one or I'll have the men take those pigs right off your truck. It proves to the government that you picked them up."

"I cain't write," he said.

"What's your name?" asked Addie.

"Leland."

"Leland what?"

"Leland Stooper."

"How do you spell it?" she asked.

"Spell what?"

The man was irksome. "Your name, Leland Stooper. Is it with two o's or a u? Do you know how to spell it?"

"I know it's my name but I cain't write it."

221

"How do you sign anything?"

"I don't. My wife signs."

"I'll tell you what," said Addie. "I am going to call the foreman over here. Then I am going to write your name, you are going to make some kind of a mark and he is going to witness it."

"Seems like a lot of trouble to haul off some pigs."

"Caleb," Addie called as he came out of the barn. "Come over here and witness this transaction."

She turned to the driver. "This paper says that you picked up the pigs today. So, if you don't get them to where the government told you to, you will have to pay for the pigs."

"That don't rightly seem fair."

"It's as fair as it gets," said Addie.

"What's the problem?" asked Caleb as he approached.

"Mr. Stooper can't write his name on this bill of sale. I want to make sure Alex gets his money."

"She says I'm gonna' pay for these pigs if they don't get where they's suppose to go."

"I want you to witness whatever mark he makes," Addie told Caleb. She wrote the man's name on the designated line, gave the driver the pen and told him to make whatever sign he could next to his name

The man took the pen and to her surprise drew the perfect picture of a pig.

"You said you couldn't write."

He gave a toothless grin. "I cain't write. I

didn't say I cain't draw."

Caleb laughed and gave the man a tap on the shoulder before he signed as a witness.

Addie checked to make sure all came through the second copy and handed it to the driver. "Give this to whoever hired you."

Caleb stood and began to jabber with the man.

Addie noticed the hired men, who loaded the pigs, stood grinning as they watched the whole sorry exchange, apparently their entertainment for the day.

She turned on her heel and marched back to the house.

CHAPTER 30

A week later, Addie was full of excitement when she received a letter from Miss Stevens relating to positions available. First item was secretarial positions in the Bureau of Navigation. Women were being recruited for Naval Coastal Defense Reserve, which meant a woman became a yeoman (F) in the navy. The navy would secure housing, maybe at the YWCA. Miss Stevens included that Addie would be responsible for her uniform which must be either blue or white with a single-breasted jacket, a skirt four inches above the ankle, and a short-brimmed hat of stiff blue felt. The enlistment was for four years!

Addie had read an article in the Winchester paper about a nurse, Anna McFadden, who had enlisted in the reserve. She had been a surgical nurse at the Garfield Memorial Hospital in Winchester and now was stationed at a base hospital in France. The paper said that over a thousand women from Virginia had signed up. Addie thought about it, but not for long. Her name was not going on any document that required four years of her life.

Next she read about numerous secretarial positions in various government offices. The pay was similar to what she earned at the farm, but she would have to pay for room and board and transportation, if she had to take a taxi or trolley.

She thought about this, too. Her debt to Alex would be paid at the end of November. She had repaid twenty of her thirty-dollars-a-month salary to him for the secretarial training, which meant little had been put into savings. Scarcity of money and more expenses meant scrimping to get by. Addie had enough of that.

Each new paragraph caused her excitement to wane until the words American Red Cross caught her eye. She had studied about Clara Barton when she was in school. The Red Cross was hiring clerical staff members. She knew a bit about the helping organization with President Woodrow Wilson as its honorary president. Uniforms and room and board were furnished to the salaried employees. If Addie got a position with the Red Cross she would be earning money, saving money, and helping with the war effort at the same time. The idea appealed to her.

Addie didn't write a return letter. She waited until it was lunch time at the school and telephoned Miss Stevens. Her former teacher was delighted. Yes, she knew one of the board members of the Red Cross and would put in a good word for Addie. When Miss Stevens knew more information she would telephone.

Mixed emotions of euphoria and doubt ran from Addie's fingers to her toes after she hung up the receiver. It was too soon to tell Lottie. Addie didn't want to tell Alex. And, what was she thinking? What was there to tell them? She didn't have a job, only the word of Miss Stevens that she would contact a person on the board.

Settling back into the affairs of Lockwood, Addie tried to push thoughts of change to the back of her mind. A cup of hot tea. That was what she needed to calm her feelings.

In the kitchen Ella was kneading dough when Addie came into the room. "I'm goin' to bake some bread for us. I like to bake bread on these kinds of days."

"Have you got water hot for tea? It's chilly in the office." Addie looked out the window. "The drizzly day seems to seep through to the bone."

"Do you think Jess would like some bread?" asked Ella.

"I'm sure he would." Addie turned to the young maid. "What are you making for supper?"

"I'm gonna' put a chicken and potatoes in the oven. There were some nice carrots in the root cellar so I'll go ahead and cook them up too."

"Why don't you go ask Jess if he would like to have supper with us? You can give him a loaf of bread to take back to his cabin."

Ella smiled. "That's a right good idea. I bet Jess gets lonesome over there by hisself."

Addie couldn't picture Jess getting lonesome but she wasn't sure. "I guess he might. He seems to be content living by himself, and he's Caleb's good friend. I'm sure Jess wouldn't pass up the chance for a good meal."

"Prob'ly so," answered Ella. "The water's hot in the teakettle. I'll fix you a cup of tea soon's I finish kneadin' this dough."

Addie had taken a mug from the cupboard and placed a tea bag in it. "I'll take care of it," she told the young girl. "Do you know where Jess is?" she asked.

"I 'spect he's around with the horses. The men don't go out to the fields on a day like this. It's kinda' like the Lord sayin' they need a rest."

Addie smiled. "I never thought of it that way. If Jess comes to eat perhaps he will stay and play cards." She looked over at the young girl. "Do you get lonesome, Ella?"

"I might if I let myself think about it but I got plenty to do in the house. You bein' here makes me feel warm and safe, and Mr. Alex comes on the weekends. Then sometimes he's haulin' in men for me to feed, so there ain't much time for me to get lonely. Besides, I jus' saw my family. I like to visit 'em, but not too often."

Ella made life seem so simple.

"Lottie and I used to spend a lot of time together," Addie mused. "Now that she and Caleb are married that has changed. I sometimes miss being in a town or having other people around."

Ella placed the big wad of dough in a greased pan and turned it over once. She put a clean dish towel over the top and sat it on top of the oven to let it rise.

"I 'spect that did change your bein' together all the time. I ain't never had a close girlfriend so I don't really know how it would be."

Addie's weak smile told the story. "Life ain't the same."

Ella's head jerked up. "You said ain't."

"I wanted to see if you would notice. From now on I expect you will use isn't instead of ain't. You know the difference."

Ella looked over at her. "I think you tricked me."

Addie picked up the cup of tea and grinned. "Ain't that the truth," she replied and went back to the office.

Ella stood with a puzzled look on her pretty face.

**

Jess was more than happy to come for supper. He wore a freshly ironed striped cotton shirt and denim pants. His face shone as bright as his polished cowboy boots. In his broad hand were two wrapped presents for the young ladies. He handed the presents to them as soon as he entered.

"Should we open them now?" asked Addie.

He was honest. "Why not wait until after we eat because I am mighty hungry and the smell of that food makes me hungrier."

"We'll eat in the kitchen," advised Addie.

"Saving the dining room for important guests?" he asked.

"It's warmer and more comfortable in the kitchen," answered Addie.

He held a smirk at the side of his mouth. "Maybe."

"I'll put the food on warm plates and bring it to the table. Anybody goin' to say grace?" questioned Ella.

"I will," offered Jess, which brought a look of surprise from the young women.

"Come sit down, Ella. We're going to hold hands while I deliver up this prayer," he ordered.

Ella did as requested and the three held hands around the table.

"Dear Lord," began Jess in his deep voice. "I thank you for the good fortune of sharing this meal with two of the loveliest ladies you have seen fit to put upon this earth. While we are safe and snug, we can't forget about the boys serving in this war we have gotten ourselves into, so we ask you to keep them safe. Finally, we thank you for the food and fellowship which we are about to enjoy. Amen."

Ella rose to bring the plates to the table. "That was right nice, Jess," she said.

"I am lax in saying my prayers," apologized Addie. "Are you sure you aren't a preacher?"

He chuckled. "That was my father. Some of it rubbed off on me, but not much."

Addie raised a questioning eye. "Are you the prodigal son?"

"Not likely." He laughed. "The most extravagant thing I've done is buy these cowboy boots."

"I noticed they are always clean and polished," said Addie.

"They're the only pair I own."

Ella set the plates of food before them and brought a basket of sliced bread to the table. "I made a loaf for you, Jess, if you want to take one back to the cabin."

"Ella, you are as sweet as you are pretty. I'd love to take a loaf with me. Some man is going to come along and sweep you off your feet."

Ella blushed a bright red. "You shouldn't say things like that."

"Why not?" he asked. "It's the truth."

Addie tried to cover Ella's embarrassment. "You are a wonderful cook, Ella, and you are a good student."

Addie turned to Jess. "Ella and I work on lessons every night."

Jess was busy with his food. "Is that right? I'm glad to hear it. Is Addie a good teacher?"

Ella's eyes lit up. "I'd say so. Isn't that right, Miss Addie?"

Addie stopped buttering a piece of bread. Isn't instead of ain't? She grinned at the young girl. "I believe I am getting the lessons across."

After clearing away the soiled dishes Addie brought a deck of cards to the table. "What card game do you know for three people to play?"

"I can teach you how to play pitch," said Jess. "But first you need to open your presents."

He didn't have to mention it again. The presents were wrapped in brown paper he'd cut from a paper bag and wrapped them with string. The two eager women could hardly wait to see what he had brought. When they did, oohs and aahs were heard.

Jess had whittled a whistle for Ella and a cow for Addie. The cow he had painted copper-red with patches of white. It was low and round just like the cattle Alex had purchased. The cow had a white face and horns, and Addie was impressed with the workmanship.

"This is beautiful, Jess. You always surprise me."

"I told you there was a lot about me you didn't know. I like to work with wood," he said. "Ella, I made that whistle so you won't have to go running to find us. It's a wooden penny whistle. You can learn to play a tune on it if you want to."

Ella blew into it and jumped at the sound. Jess showed her how to cover the holes to make different sounds.

Ella was confused. "How will anybody know who I'm whistling for?"

"Work out a call for each of us. Maybe one long one for Caleb, two short ones for me, a different one for Addie. You just tell us what we need to listen for."

"You sure are smart, Jess," Ella said. She blew on the penny whistle, amazed at the sounds she could make.

Addie scrunched her face at the sound. She wasn't so sure about Ella's gift. Jess held a wide satisfied smile.

He showed them card tricks and taught them how to play pitch. They played for an hour before

Jess decided it was time to leave. He tucked Ella's loaf of bread under his arm.

Addie walked him to the door. "I'm glad you came, Jess. When the weather is like this, the days are long. Any more thoughts about going back to Oklahoma?"

"Not just yet," he answered. "How about you, Addie? You're too young to be stuck on this farm forever. It would be different if you were married."

"I came here as a favor to Alex," she replied.

"He's a fool," he said.

"Jess, don't be unkind. Alex has been good to me."

"Good to himself," he complained. "If I were him, I'd have you hitched to my cart a long time ago."

Addie made a prune face. "Maybe I don't want to be hitched."

"You would if Alex owned the cart," he retorted.

"Maybe times will change, Jess."

"When Hell freezes over," he said. He kissed her hand. "Night, Addie. I had a good time."

"So did I. Night, Jess."

In the kitchen, Ella was tooting on that penny whistle. "Listen to this, Miss Addie." She blew four different notes and grinned with her new-found skill.

"Very nice," complimented Addie. "I hope you don't have to use that thing too often."

CHAPTER 31

It was settled. The Board of Directors was satisfied with Addie's educational records along with recommendations from both Miss Stevens and the director of the secretarial school. Addie was to arrive in Washington to begin training on November 1st.

She wasn't prepared for how the news was received by others.

Lottie wasn't pleased. "I knew you would be off again, but I had hoped it would be after the baby is born. What if I need you? You won't be here for me."

She had hoped Lottie would be happy for her.

Maybe the unexpected response was due to carrying a baby. Addie had heard that women acted differently when they were in the family way.

Addie gave Lottie the benefit of the doubt. "You have Caleb and there is a telephone in the house."

"It won't be the same," countered Lottie.

Addie knew what she meant. "Perhaps I won't like the Red Cross or Washington, and I will turn around and come back. I can't pass up this opportunity."

"You don't know what you want." Then Lottie acquiesced, "I guess it's like us going to

Colorado. If we hadn't gone we would always wonder if we should have."

Jess had been encouraging. "I think you're making a good decision. You'll be right in the middle of where all the decisions are made." He gave her a sketch of Lockwood he had drawn. There it was: the big white stucco house with the stone steps leading up to the wide porch, the house where Caleb and Lottie live, Jess's cabin by the Buckmarsh Run, and the fields and fencing that seemed to go on forever. "This will help you recall fond memories."

He was right. The drawing seemed to leap off the paper. One more facet of Jess that Addie had never seen. She remembered he had said there was a lot to him that she didn't know, which she thought he said to impress her. She was beginning to believe him.

Addie broke the news to Alex while they were in the office. He sat as though he had been put into a trance.

She intended to lessen the impact of her announcement of leaving. "I have given this much thought, Alex. The winter farm affairs are not as demanding. It will give you time to hire someone else if needed."

He wasn't pleased. "I was planning on closing my law practice by the first of the year."

"Why will my absence interfere with that? I thought you were going to close it months ago."

"I wanted to be on solid footing before I went forward with future plans," Alex told her.

Addie found his words irksome. "You never included me in those plans. If you had, perhaps I wouldn't have accepted this position."

His troubled brown eyes looked directly at her. "I didn't feel it was necessary. The timing wasn't right."

Addie rose from her chair. "I know your financial obligations and this place has been able to pay for itself almost from the beginning. Once you close that law office that keeps you captive, I'm sure you can go ahead with any plans you have in mind. And, if you get in a bind, call Plain Jane. She watches over you like a mother hen."

Alex raised his eyebrows. "I don't understand why you're upset."

"I'm sure you don't." She turned on her heel and left the room.

She felt pushed from every angle. Her mother said it was a foolish venture because she had a fine job. Her pa said whatever she thought best, and Aunt Lilly said she wished she could have done something like that when she was young.

Only Jess had encouraged her decision.

Addie's room was neat and tidy when she finished packing. She left a few personal items behind for when she came to visit. Alex was going to take her to the Bluemont train station in his Franklin. Addie was a bundle of nerves when she latched her suitcase.

Alex waited in the foyer looking dapper in his camelhair coat and brown fedora. Before he picked up her suitcase, he put on brown leather gloves. "It's chilly out. Are you going to be warm enough?"

"I'll be fine," she answered.

Ella came from the kitchen. "Miss Addie, I'm so sorry you're leavin' us."

"I'll come back to visit, Ella." She hugged the sad young girl and looked at Alex. "That is if Mr. Alex will allow me to come."

"You will always have a spot here," he answered.

Welcome words.

When they reached Bluemont, after a quiet trip and listening to Alex talk about his Hereford/ Aberdeen Angus cattle, Addie felt tears welling up. She had given this change in her life a lot of thought, but the act of doing it gave her mixed feelings. She wouldn't see the new calves, or lambs, or Caleb and Lottie's baby. Jess may be gone by the time she came for a visit. There might be a new girl sitting in her chair in the office and working closely with Alex. Most of all, she would miss Lockwood. She had grown to love the place.

Alex looked over at her. "You're quiet," he observed.

She could only nod her head.

"I want you to call me as soon as you are settled. Reverse the charges."

She nodded again.

"We will be lost without you," he said.

We. How about you, Alex? Will you be lost without me, she wondered.

By the time the Franklin climbed the curvy mountain road to Bluemont, Addie had composed herself. She had made this decision and she would go ahead. Alex pulled the car to the side of the narrow road leading to the station. He pulled her suitcase from the back seat.

"I'll check and see if the train is on time," he offered.

"No," said Addie. "I will sit and wait if it is late in arriving."

Alex pulled an envelope from his pocket. "Here's a letter from Clay for you to read on the train. It came yesterday and I forgot to give it to you. I just realized it was in my pocket. Sorry."

A wan smile appeared on her face. "It's probably better for me to read it today than yesterday. I worry about Clay."

"We all do," he replied. "Let's hope this war is over soon. Addie what are your true feelings for Clay?"

The question surprised her. "He is a friend. I thought you knew that."

"He hopes to marry you one day, Addie. He told me."

Is that the reason Alex has been all business and not made one move as if he cared for her? He has been a different Alex than the man she knew in Colorado, or did she misjudge him?

"When people marry, it is because they are both in agreement," she answered.

He nodded as if he understood.

The train whistle announced its arrival. Addie had her ticket. "Right on time," she said. "I can take my suitcase."

"No. I will carry it to the conductor. You will be on your own at the end of the line. Promise you will call as soon as you can."

"I promise."

He handed her suitcase to the conductor on the platform and walked her to the railcar. Before she boarded, he pulled her close. "I hope you find what you're searching for."

Addie's mind was swimming.

When he let her go, she couldn't look at him. Her legs felt rubbery as she went up the metal steps. "Good bye, Alex," she mumbled.

He didn't say anything. He didn't even watch to see the train pull away. A dejected Alex walked back to his Franklin touring car where he sat for a long moment before he turned the auto onto the lonesome road back to Lockwood.

CHAPTER 32

As soon as she dabbed the tears away that had squeezed out of the corners of her eyes, Addie opened Clay's letter.

October 21, 1917

My dear Addie,

I find myself in France. We landed here after a sometimes choppy ride over the ocean, and docked at Brest. We spent one week in that dirty city where we were housed in a hayloft. There were four of us who shared a spot in the mow and have become buddies.

Now, we are known by nicknames: Slick is from New York City, said he's been on his own since he was ten, Bruiser is from Tennessee, I think his name tells you all, Squirrel is a little guy from North Carolina, he can shimmy up a rope faster than I've ever seen. They call me Professor because I went to college. Slick, of the three, probably went the farthest in school, which was third grade. His street knowledge astounds me.

We are part of an eight-man rifle squad, but the four of us have assigned ourselves various duties not related to the army. Slick is to make sure we don't get snookered when playing cards or rolling dice, Bruiser handles any disputes, Squirrel is a master at obtaining extra food, and I interpret everything given to us in writing. The directions for caring for and assembling a rifle with a bayonet were taxing. Bruiser said, "Heck, I ben handlin' and puttin' guns together all my life. This one's jus' fancier." We are now all well-versed on the rifle.

This way of life is all new to me, but I am learning much about the world that I wouldn't have learned at the university. I have decided that I will finish out my college year when I return and perhaps go into the field of medicine. I have seen many of the wounded allied troops. It is enough to break your heart.

We are now at Neufchateau, where the division headquarters are being constructed. The four of us will stay together and we are sharing a tent with four cots. It seems a luxury after the week in the hayloft. It is a busy time. When the headquarters are finished the place will be like a small city, a tent city, that is.

Here is the most remarkable news of all. My commanding officer is Major Asa Thomas from Virginia. He is from the Suffolk area, but his wife used to be Dr. Hawthorne's nurse for a short time. I do not know her. He tells me there is another major here from our home county of Clarke. I have yet to meet him.

The rain has been relentless and chills to the bone. Many of our troops are down with dysentery and pneumonia. There are thousands of men here from different countries so the likelihood of picking up some kind of sickness bug is ever present. We have a base hospital that used to be a nunnery. It is filled more with illnesses and accidents than war injuries.

We are receiving training from the French. There are no orders as to when we will be sent to relieve allied troops. I'm hoping we are well-trained by that time. The threat of poison gas and fighting in trenches does not appeal to me at the present.

In short, I will be glad when this war is over and I can return to American soil. We don't appreciate what we have until we don't have it.

I think of home and you often. They are good memories that keep me going. I know you don't think of me as I do of you, but I keep the hope alive that one day that will change.

Please write and give me the news. I do get homesick.

> *Affectionately,*
> *Clay*

Addie folded the letter, put it in her pocketbook and snapped it shut. She wondered if Clay was cut out to be in the service. She couldn't picture him with a gun and bayonet aiming to strike down another fellow human being. Clay was too kind and gentle for that. She also wondered how this war would affect him.

Letting a sigh drift out, she looked out the cloudy window of the train. The conductor said they would be in Leesburg in five minutes for a fifteen minute stop. There would be time to visit a lavatory and pick up a refreshment for those who chose to do so. Addie welcomed the news. Clay's letter had not been uplifting. She could do with a bottle of pop.

In Leesburg, an elder gentleman took the empty seat beside her. He smiled at Addie when he sat down and snored all the way to Alexandria. She hadn't felt like carrying on a conversation and was spared the effort.

The Alexandria train station was familiar from her days at the secretarial school. She knew where to get a taxi and instruct the driver to take her to the boarding house, where Miss Stevens had reserved a room for her.

"I know the place," said the hackie. "Lucky you've got a place because people are flooding into Washington and places to stay are scarce." He took her suitcase and placed it on the back seat next to her. "Are you going to be working in the city? Lots of women are working now that we're in the war. I'm too old for the army or I'd be right in there with those boys."

Addie didn't need his apology. She needed to get to the rooming house. Her nerves were on edge.

After a half-hour the taxi stopped in front of a brick house in a series of brick townhouses. He came around to get her suitcase. She paid the fare and stood looking at the townhouse as the hackie drove away. There was a series of cement steps up to the door. She climbed up the stair lugging her suitcase and rang the bell.

A middle-aged tall lady with brown hair streaked with gray came to the door. Addie introduced herself and the reason she was there.

"I am Eleanor Hopkins. This is my home and I am renting rooms to assist with the war effort. There are three other roomers on the second floor where you will be staying and one on the third floor. The rules of the house are printed and attached to the back of the door. I do not provide meals, only the lodging. I understand you will be working for the American Red Cross, which I believe to be a noble organization. That is the reason I agreed when Miss Stevens called me. Here is the key. Your room is Number Three. I occupy this level. If you encounter any problems, shove a note under my door."

The woman was a far cry from her former landlady, the kind Mrs. Tygert of Leadville, Colorado.

"Miss Hopkins, you said Miss Stevens called. Do you have a telephone I can use?"

"The telephone you may use is on the wall in the second level. You must pay for long distance calls. The use of the telephone for local calling is included in the rent. Had you gone up to your room you would have seen this information posted in the "Rules of the Room".

"Thank you," came Addie's quiet reply. She climbed up one flight of stairs and looked for Room Three. It was the second door to the left. The door key was heavy and cumbersome, but she managed to open the door after a fashion.

Before her was the four-dollar-a-week room. A twin-sized maple bed with a short headboard sat in a corner covered with a plain cream-colored spread. One pillow with a matching pillowcase. There was a maple dresser with three drawers, a dry sink with a washbowl and ewer, one cream-colored washcloth, face towel and bath towel. She did have a small desk and chair. The room was plain but adequate. All of a sudden, she realized there was no window. How could she live without having a window to air out the room or look out at the world? She feared it would be like living in a cell. Addie surveyed the room once more. What she had thought the Red Cross would pay for turned out to be her obligation. She had to pay four dollars a week for this windowless room, plus food and transportation. The realization caused her to fall on the bed and sob her heart out.

Two hours later she felt composed enough to call Alex without breaking down. The phone was on the wall a few feet from her room. There certainly wouldn't be any privacy when using this phone. Addie took the receiver off the side of the box and dialed the operator. She gave the phone number of Lockwood and Alex's name and told the operator to reverse the charges.

When Alex answered she wanted to shout, "Come and get me!" Instead she said, "Hi Alex. I told you I would call when I was settled."

"Is everything all right?" he asked. "You sound distant."

"I am distant," she tried to be upbeat.

"Not in that way. Are you sure you are all right?"

"I am. Just tired. I have a room in a townhouse about three blocks from where I will be working. I can take the trolley when the weather is bad."

"We had a dusting of snow here this afternoon. How is the weather in Washington?"

"Raw, damp and cold," she answered. "I have to go out and see if there is a store nearby. The lady who runs this house doesn't include meals. I haven't read all of the rules of the house so perhaps we are allowed to use the kitchen. It is a whole new world, Alex."

"And one that I hope you will tire of soon," he said.

"I haven't even started work. I will be sure to keep you informed. I read Clay's letter."

"How is he?" asked Alex.

"I believe he is liking what he is learning. He's found a group of buddies, but still he gets homesick, which is to be expected. He is thousands of miles away in France," she told him. "I understand what it feels like because I had those pangs of loneliness when Lottie and I were in Colorado."

"You never told me that."

"It wasn't necessary," she replied. "I overcame them. Alex, I had better say goodbye because this will be an expensive call."

"You are worth it," he replied. "I want you to call me once a week unless you need to contact me earlier. What is the number there?"

245

Addie read it off. "I will call. Tell Lottie that my room is a tad bigger than the one we shared at Mrs. Tygert's." Addie wanted to add that this landlady wasn't nearly as nice and friendly as Mrs. Tygert, but she was afraid someone would hear her, so she kept it to herself.

After she hung up the phone she went back to her room and read the rules posted on the back of the door. The boarders were allowed to use the kitchen between the hours of seven and nine in the morning and five and seven in the evenings. At least she wouldn't starve.

CHAPTER 33

Addie reported to Walter Reed Army Hospital at eight o'clock the next morning. She went up the steps of the brick building where a receptionist guided her to a waiting room. Other young women were seated and looking as at out of place as she felt.

After a few minutes an official looking woman came into the room. "Welcome to the American Red Cross," she said. "Those of you who have been accepted into the clerical corps, follow me." Addie rose from her seat and three other women joined her.

"This is orientation day," announced the leader. "You will be informed about the organization, goals, and functioning of the Red Cross. After that you will receive lunch and be measured for uniforms." Uniforms?

"The last two hours of the day will be spent on the clerical duties you have been assigned," informed the supervisor.

Addie thought this must be similar to being in the military. There was so much information to absorb she had written notes in shorthand so she could study them when she returned to the boarding house.

At lunchtime the women introduced themselves. Only one of them was close to Addie's age, but she was a snob. "I am planning on an important position because my parents are quite influential. I am only here to help in the war effort. I wanted to volunteer, but Father said I might as well get paid for the work."

Another woman spoke up. "As for me, I had little choice," she allowed. "I have two children to feed and a husband in the army."

The third woman, who looked to be in her thirties, said, "I am not married and I am looking forward to a long career. I chose the American Red Cross because it is helping both in the war and here at home. I taught school for a time but discovered that was not my calling."

It was Addie's turn. She told them she was a graduate of a secretarial school and that she had seen to the financial affairs of a big estate. She didn't add that she was ready for a change because, what she had hoped would blossom into a lasting relationship with Alex Lockwood, was a fantasy of hers. She had to get away.

The four had nothing in common except becoming a member in the clerical corps. Where was Lottie when she needed her?

At five o'clock, after the orientation and tests of their secretarial skills, they were assigned positions. Addie was given the appointment of secretary to the Director of Outreach, which meant little to her at the time.

When their respective positions were announced, the snobbish girl spoke up. "I'm sure there has been a mistake. My appointment is to the typing pool."

The supervisor looked over the information. "There has been no mistake."

With a toss of head, she said, "I shall leave. I am far above the mindless job as a typist."

Addie smiled inwardly. She thought that a good decision because she had witnessed the girl's efforts at typing.

On the way to Walter Reed, Addie had seen a small grocery store on one of the side streets. The only provisions she had at the townhouse were some tea bags and a jar of peanut butter. She had seen the kitchen, which was equipped with a double burner kerosene stove and an ice box. When she opened that door she found little room in it to store foods that needed refrigeration. Jars, bottles and cartons were labeled with people's names on them. She would have to be cautious about what she purchased.

Addie entered the small store, which carried not only groceries but an assortment of necessary items. It was like Mr. White's general store in Berryville only half the size. She bought a quart of milk, one can of Campbell's noodle soup, a loaf of bread, a jar of Smucker's strawberry jam, an orange and a package of Fig Newtons. The only item to go into the ice box was the quart of milk.

Addie thanked Mr. Groves, the store owner. He was short with dark hair greying at the temples and rather nice-looking for a man in middle age, thought Addie. "I'm sure I will be stopping by quite often," she said.

"Are you new to the area? I'm familiar with most of my customers."

"Yes, I just moved here."

"New faces every day," he told her. "Lots of jobs now that we're in the war. Bringing people from all over the country."

When Addie returned to the boarding house, there was another young lady mounting the steps. She turned when she saw Addie behind her. "Let me hold the door. You have your arms full."

"Thanks," answered Addie. "I had to pick up some groceries."

"Are you living here?" asked the girl as she held the door.

"Yes, I'm in room three."

"My name is Fannie Quain. I am renting the attic." She made a wry face.

They stood in the hall. "I'm Adelaide Richards. People call me Addie."

"I'm glad to know you," said Fannie. "Can I help you with something?"

"No thanks. I only have to put milk in the ice box."

The door to the side of them opened. "What is this noise?" asked Eleanor, the landlady.

"Addie and I just met," Fannie answered.

"Now that you have, get on to your rooms without disturbing the whole house." She stepped back into her room and closed the door.

Fannie whispered. "She is a pain in the derriere. Come up to my room later."

"I will," Addie whispered back.

Addie decided to let the soup heat on the stove while she carried the other groceries to her room. When she returned the soup was hot. In the cupboard was a small teapot that was perfect to carry the soup to her room. Addie didn't like the feel of the kitchen. Her thoughts turned to the warm kitchen at Lockwood with the wood stove and Ella fussing about. They had enjoyed many cups of hot tea and pleasant conversation in that room. But she wasn't at Lockwood, she was in a townhouse in Washington. Addie was glad she met Fannie. Once she ate her dinner of soup, peanut butter and jam sandwich, she would call on the spritely girl who lived in the attic.

CHAPTER 34

Fannie Quain was an Irish young lady who had lived in the city all of her eighteen years. She worked as a waitress in a café and cleaned house for a lady who lived in a mansion two blocks away. Fannie was a bundle of energy, an appealing lass with flaming-red hair and emerald-green eyes that were as lively as she was.

Addie knocked on the door.

"Come on in here," greeted Fannie. "I've been waiting for you."

"I had supper before I came up."

"Good, I'll fix us each an Irish whiskey."

Addie's eyebrows flew up. "Whiskey? I don't drink except for a small glass of wine on special occasions."

"This is a special occasion and I like whiskey. It'll help you unwind. I have a glass every evening. Lord knows, I need it after the days I put in."

Addie sat in an upholstered arm chair. She looked around the attic room with its wooden beams showing. Big nails had been driven into the beams, which Fannie used to hang baskets, buckets, cleaning supplies, and dresses and hats. Her cot was in a corner under the eaves and various boxes held other articles. There was a flowered chair that matched the one Addie was sitting in. One window under the peak of the roof let in light.

"Can you open that window?"

"Yes, but it doesn't have a screen. One day I found a bat hanging on one of those beams and a pigeon who thought this was a bathroom, so I don't open it unless it's stifling and I'm here."

"How long have you lived here?" asked Addie. "It must be unbearable in the summer."

Fannie handed her a jigger of whiskey and sat in the flowered chair next to her. "I moved in three months ago. My mother said I had a choice, either move out or get married. Well, I looked around at how she lived with a husband always at the pub and a trail of little ones under her feet and I moved out. Besides, I didn't have any steady boyfriend. This is a good part of the city and the rent is only two-fifty a week."

Addie chuckled, "And, you have a window."

Fannie nodded at her. "Just sip that stuff or it'll burn your gullet. What about you, Addie? Where'd you come from?"

Addie gave her the story of graduating high school, spending time in Colorado, training a year at the secretarial school, working at Lockwood, and her new position with the Red Cross.

Fannie was enraptured with her tale. "I can't believe you'd leave a place like that to come to the city. Must be something that made you leave."

Addie wasn't about to tell Fannie about her feelings for Alex. "I get itchy feet," she answered.

253

"Go ahead, take a sip of that whiskey. It'll warm your toes and stop a cold."

"I had some brandy once," admitted Addie. "I didn't like the taste of it but it did warm me up. I don't like this damp cold weather."

Fannie smiled, "Guess I'm used to it. I've never been out of the city."

Addie was surprised. "You will have to come out with me to visit Lockwood."

"I'd like that. When will you go?" asked Fannie.

"Maybe at Christmas. Of course, I will have to check with Alex to see if that would be agreeable."

"Is he the man who owns the big place?" Fannie wanted to know.

"Yes," said Addie. "You can meet my best friend Lottie, she lives on the farm. She's going to have a baby in the spring. Her husband Caleb is foreman for the farm and his friend, Jess..." she stopped. "Oh, Fannie. We could have such a good time."

Was it the few sips of whiskey or the thoughts of Lockwood farm that put her in a mellow mood? It didn't matter. Addie felt the most uplifted she had since she arrived in Washington.

She would call Alex next week, as he had asked her to, and pose the question of bringing Fannie for a visit at Christmastime. The thought of Lockwood and Christmas gave Addie a boost.

"I had better get back to my room," Addie told Fannie. "I have a lot of notes to study before I go to work tomorrow."

"I wish I was smart like you. I quit school early to help my mother."

"Fannie, I expect you are smarter than me in many ways. Will I see you tomorrow?"

"I have to work at the café the next couple of days and won't get home until about ten in the evening. Maybe on Friday night we could go out to eat. I know a place that serves up a good plate of fish and chips," proposed Fannie.

"Fish and chips? I've never had any."

"You're in for a treat," said Fannie. "We'll wash them down with Irish beer."

"I believe I'll stick with tea," answered Addie, who was feeling lightheaded from the alcohol.

Fannie laughed. "It's sure you didn't grow up with the Irish. Friday night at six o'clock."

"I'll be waiting," said Addie, and went down the attic stairs to room three. The room without a window.

CHAPTER 35

Friday evening Addie waited for Fannie to knock on her door. She discovered being secretary to the Director of Outreach was a demanding job. The hours were from eight until five with an hour for lunch. She couldn't find time for lunch so she packed a sandwich and worked until quitting time, which was becoming five-thirty or six instead of five.

The American Red Cross worked in tandem with the International Red Cross and were involved in setting up hospitals, schools, orphanages, and providing relief for soldiers of every country involved in the war. The organization wasn't on any side of the war, it was there to help.

As secretary, Addie was involved with everything that came to the attention of the director. Her responsibility was to get the information to him and designated workers such as typists, accountants and schedulers. Once they returned the finished product to her, she was to check it over before handing it to the director. If she found a mistake, back it went for correction to be reviewed once again.

By the end of each day she was drained of energy. No wonder Fannie had a shot of whiskey every night. Addie didn't need whiskey. She was so tired she fell into bed, sometimes without supper.

Fannie's knock startled her. "I think I was falling asleep," she said to her friend.

"I'm dead," Fannie responded. "But, I've got enough life to get us to the best fish and chips in the city."

"How far is it? Do we need to take a taxi?"

Fannie's green eyes opened wide. "A taxi? Who's got money for that? We'll take the trolley, although they're getting almost as expensive."

Addie locked her door and they went down the flight of stairs.

"The old sourpuss will be listening to see what time we get back," Fannie whispered as they went out the door.

"How does she know who's in the hall?"

"Believe me, she knows. The other women in the house are dried up grapes. You can set your clock by them," informed Fannie.

"I haven't run into them," said Addie.

"They're like mice," said Fannie. "Sneak in and out of their rooms. What they need is a night on the town."

The trolley arrived at the stop a few minutes after they did.

Fannie boarded first. "Hey, Mitch. How's it going?" she said to the driver.

"Going out for a big night, Fannie? Who's your friend?" replied Mitch.

"She's a country girl and smart as they come so you'd better not try any funny stuff."

257

The driver guffawed. "I'd be hard-put to get anything past you, Miss Fannie Quain. How's your ma?"

"She told me to get out of the house or get married. The only handsome guy I know is you and you're already married so I got out of the house."

Addie couldn't believe what she was hearing. Mitch was at least fifty, red-faced and round as a balloon. Addie's eyes were downcast from embarrassment because she saw the other passengers watching and listening. It was a relief when they took seats.

Fannie leaned toward her. "I've known Mitch since I was little. I saw that look on your face, do I embarrass you?"

"I'm not inclined to be as vocal as you are," answered Addie.

Fannie laughed. "That's a good one. I'll try to act like a lady. They give coy smiles and polite how-do-you-dos."

Addie smiled over at her. "Just be yourself, Fannie. I'm looking forward to those fish and chips."

What Addie expected to be a restaurant turned out to be an Irish pub in the basement of one of the big buildings in a run-down part of the city. The room had chairs and tables on one side and a bar on the other. Addie was glad she hadn't worn the smart green suit Lottie had made for her. She would have been out of place. Noisy men sat at the bar in their grimy work clothes drinking and smoking.

Fannie went to an unoccupied table farthest away from the bar. Addie could feel the men eyeing them as they walked to that spot. One man called, "Hey Fannie, who's that pretty miss behind you?"

Fannie looked over. "Watch yourself, Eddie. She's got a husband twice your size."

The other men laughed and slapped him on the back.

A waitress came to their table. "Fannie, you ain't bin around here for a spell. Where you keepin' yourself?"

"In the nicer part of town," she answered. "This is my friend, Addie."

The waitress nodded to Addie. "Hey Addie," she said. "I'm Lucy. We're busier than a hive of bees tonight."

"We're going to have the fish and chips and a couple of stout ales," ordered Fannie before Addie could say a word.

In an apron that once was white and now a dishwater gray, the frayed Lucy turned and headed for the kitchen. Addie looked around the noisy, smoky room then looked over at Fannie. "Do you come here often?" she asked.

"I was raised in this section. The men work hard and then spend a lot of their money in the bars when their wives wish they would bring the paycheck home. I wanted to get out of here."

Addie was puzzled. "Why did we come?"

"Because I wanted you to see the area where I grew up, and the food is the best. I don't feel like I fit in the nicer Washington restaurants. Just like

259

you don't feel like you fit here." She watched to see how Addie would respond.

Addie shrugged. "I grew up in a tenant house with two brothers and a baby sister I had to help bring into the world."

Fannie was surprised. "I never figured that," she said. "You've had an education and you have an important job. And, it sounds like the big farm you worked at before you came here is a ritzy place."

Addie was wistful recalling the image of Lockwood. "I would call it stately. The man who owns it is a lawyer. If the farm works out the way he hopes, it could be a showplace once he dresses up the inside. Right now, it needs a new coat of paint on the walls and new furnishings. I have a picture in my room that Jess drew for me. I'll show it to you."

"Jess," said Fannie. "Is he the cowboy?"

"Was a cowboy. Now he's a hired hand until he decides to go back to Oklahoma. He is something to watch the way he works the horses and the cattle."

"Do you like him as a boyfriend?" asked Fannie.

Addie shook her head and smiled. "No. I don't have a boyfriend. Do you?"

"I used to. He was always talking about getting married, and then I found out he was going out with two other girls, so I ditched him quick."

Lucy brought two big plates of food and the ale. "Eat and drink hearty," she said and dropped the tab before she left.

Addie stared at her plate of breaded fish and crisp potatoes. "This is enough for two people."

Fannie was already forking fish into her mouth. "I haven't eaten good in a week."

"Neither have I," agreed Addie. After a tentative moment, she took a bite and savored the flavor. "Oh, Fannie, you are right this is delicious."

Fannie laughed. "Told you so."

They not only finished all the food on their plates but all the ale in the large glasses. By the time they returned to the townhouse they were in a spirited mood.

"Let's go knock on Ol' Eleanor Hopkins door and yell, fire," said Fannie.

Addie laughed, "That would cause an uproar and she'd put us out on our ears."

Fannie changed her mind. "Guess that's not such a hot idea. Once we get up the stairs, you can lock yourself in your cell and I'll try to make it to my lavish room in the attic."

Addie laughed again. "That ale was too much for me. I don't think I can say that word… lavith…lavith. Nope, I can't."

"No more Irish ale for you, Miss Addie."

They went up the front steps and the flight to Addie's room, trying not to disturb the landlady. Fannie helped Addie unlock her door, said good night and headed for the attic stairs.

Addie changed into her nightgown and fell fast asleep.

CHAPTER 36

On Saturday, Addie awoke with a headache. She took two aspirins to relieve the discomfort. It must be cold outdoors because her room felt chilly. The room was heated with an iron radiator using steam heat, which she had no means of regulating.

She went to the kitchen and made a cup of hot tea. It was too much trouble to toast a piece of bread in a pan over the burner of the kerosene stove so she buttered a piece of plain bread for her breakfast. She wasn't hungry after the big plate of fish and chips last evening, but her stomach was a tad queasy and some food may relieve the feeling.

Addie wondered if Fannie woke up with a headache because she was going to work all day at the café and that would mean a double headache. Fannie didn't like waitress work.

Addie took the tea and the bread to her room. She owed Clay a letter. Sipping tea, she sat in the small arm chair, exactly like the two in the attic, and waited until the effects of the aspirin relieved the thumping in her head. There would be no more Irish ale for her.

When she felt better, she sat at the desk and pulled a sheet of stationery before her.

December 5, 1917

Dear Clay,

I received your letter almost a week ago. Alex gave it to me to read on the train. I am pleased that you have pals in the army. You describe them in such a way that I can only believe they are an unconventional sort.

I am writing from my rented room in Washington, D.C. It is nothing to brag about. I have joined the clerical corps of the American Red Cross and this townhouse is within three blocks of Walter Reed Army Hospital, where the Red Cross headquarters are located.

I am the secretary to the Director of Outreach. The pay is the same as Alex paid me at Lockwood. I retired my debt to him, which left me little in the way of savings. In this house I must pay for my room and meals, but I am provided a work uniform so that saves on clothing expenses, which I figure will even out in the long run.

I joined up to help in the war effort and also for the families who are struggling now that men are being conscripted into the military. In fact, one of the women who joined when I did has two children to support. She is fortunate to be living with her parents, who take care of the children in her absence. I am glad I don't have that responsibility.

I have met a lively Irish girl who rents the attic. Fannie was born here in the city. She is not pretty but attractive, close to my height and size with red hair, green eyes, a sprinkling of freckles. Fannie's zest for life is intoxicating. She and I went

*for fish and chips last evening at an Irish pub. I had
never been in a pub. I looked about to be sure there
wasn't anyone who would recognize me. I have to
tell you the meal was most enjoyable. I also had
a tall glass of Irish ale. My head is telling me this
morning that will be my last glass.*

*You are probably thinking this is not the
Adelaide I know, and you are right. I am hoping this
position with the Red Cross will open me up to the
wider world. Just as you are, Clay, I am learning
there is much outside of our Clarke County.*

*I do miss Lottie. I can no longer run over
to her house whenever the spirit moves me. Her
marriage has altered our relationship, but she
will always remain my best friend and confidant.
I miss Ella in the kitchen, seeing the horses in the
fields and the wide vista from the front porch of
Lockwood. This room doesn't even have a window.
The radiator is either too hot or too cold. The
landlady who runs this place, Eleanor Hopkins, is
almost as cold as the radiator, but I will stick it out
for as long as I can.*

*I am thinking of visiting Lockwood at
Christmastime. If Alex gives permission, I plan to
have Fannie accompany me. She has never been to
the country. It isn't the prettiest time of year, but I
think she would enjoy getting out of the city for a
couple of days.*

*I do not look forward to the train rides
because they are long, boring and uncomfortable.*

*I think it is wonderful that your commanding
officer is Virginia born. Perhaps by now you have*

been introduced to the officer from Clarke County.
I believe the Lord is watching out for you and pray
He will keep you safe until you return home.

Your friend,
Addie

She folded the letter with a wistful sigh and thoughts of Clay. She could envision them as children playing on the farm when they were young. Now Clay was in France and she was in Washington embarking on a new career. Life changes.

Addie rested most of the day. The week at work had been tiring, and she was sure the coming week would be the same. She did have to make a trip to the grocery store.

Fannie should be home around six o'clock. Addie opened her door ajar with the chain on the lock fastened. When she heard footsteps on the stairs, she unhooked the chain and went to greet Fannie.

"Hi Fannie. I waited to have supper until you came home."

"Hi Addie. What a day, I've had. What's on your mind for supper?"

"Vegetable soup. Mrs. Groves, at the grocery, made a big pot and they were selling it in quart jars. I can't eat all of it and there isn't room in the icebox. She also made cherry tarts so I bought a couple of them, too," Addie told her.

"Let me run up to my so-called room first and I'll meet you in the kitchen."

Addie went down to the kitchen to heat up the soup. A little lady was using the stove. She was frying potatoes and looked neither right nor left. Her skin was wrinkled like a prune, her hair pulled back into a severe bun. She wore a cotton dress, sweater, ankle socks and laced shoes with a two-inch heel.

Addie sat on a wood chair holding the jar of vegetable soup. If the lady would move, she could light the other burner and put on the soup to heat. "Excuse me, ma'am," she said in her kindest voice. There was no response so she said in a louder tone, "Ma'am?"

The woman never made a sign of recognition and continued frying the potatoes. When she was done, she piled them onto a plate, turned off the stove, and left the room leaving the frying pan on the burner.

Addie removed it to the sink and placed another pan over the heat into which she poured the homemade vegetable soup.

Fannie came around the corner into the kitchen.

"I see you must have met one of the weird ones. She was going up the stairs with her plate of potatoes. I think that's all she eats," said Fannie.

"Is she deaf?"

"No. She's strange, odd, may be cuckoo. The other two are just like her. I think Mrs. Hopkins gets extra money to let them stay here. Anyway, they don't bother anybody. How's the soup look?" asked Fannie. "It smells great."

"We can take it up to my room if you want."

"Is your room warm?" asked Fannie. "Mine is like an icebox."

Addie was taken aback. "Don't you have heat in the attic?"

"No. I leave the door to the stairs open and let what heat is there to waft on up."

Addie poured the soup into two big pottery mugs. She washed up the pan she'd cooked it in and left the pan on the sideboard to dry.

Fannie had her mug of soup in her hand. "If you don't have soda crackers to go with this, I have some in my attic."

"I have crackers in my room. Let's hurry before this gets too cool."

Up the stairs they went with their steaming mugs. Addie had not locked the door.

"Your room feels good," said Fannie.

"It does now, but it took some time to warm up. By bedtime, it'll probably be stifling. I wish there was a way to regulate the thing." Addie rolled back the desk cover and brought out a box of soup crackers which they dropped into their soup.

They sat side by side on Addie's bed.

Fannie had surveyed the room. "You've got a transom over the door," she observed. "Why don't you open and close that to get some circulation in here?"

"I would, but it's too high for me to reach even if I stand on the chair."

267

Fannie finished her soup and eyed the transom window. "I'm only a couple inches taller than you so I won't be able to reach it either."

"Isn't there supposed to be some long hook to catch the handle and raise it?" asked Addie.

Fannie was determined. "Let's go poke around Icy Eleanor's stuff stored in the back of the attic. Maybe there's something there we can use."

"Icy Eleanor?" Addie questioned.

Fannie scoffed. "My name for the landlady, she's so warmhearted."

"You shouldn't call her that. Maybe she's had some difficult times in her life," said an empathetic Addie.

"Haven't we all?" said Fannie. "I may only be eighteen but I've learned life never promises a smooth ride. We roll with the punches. My Irish pop said, "Fannie, God is good, but don't dance in the boat.""

Addie laughed. "I've never heard that."

"The Irish are full of all kinds of sayings," replied Fannie, "most of them dealing with life." She looked over at Addie and smiled. "Maybe that's why they drink so much."

"Come on," Addie urged. "Let's see what Icy Eleanor hides in the attic besides you."

CHAPTER 37

Not only did they find a long pole with a hook that fit under the handle of the transom window, but they moved Fannie's cot into Addie's room. Addie couldn't bear to think of her friend sleeping in an unheated area of the attic. The addition of the cot caused the room to be almost as crowded as the room she shared with Lottie in Mrs. Tygert's boarding house. But, there was enough room to walk between the beds.

Fannie left her other belongings in the attic. Each evening she brought the clothes she would wear to work to Addie's room so they wouldn't be like icicles. Both young women had long work days and were tired out when they arrived home.

It was well into the next week before Addie called Alex. After the operator gave them the go ahead, after she reversed the charges, he said, "Are you all right Adelaide? You were supposed to call a few days ago and I have been worried."

"You have the phone number, you could have called." She didn't want to say that. "I'm sorry. That was unkind. I have had busy days and I'm so tired when I get home I can barely stay awake."

"Are you ready to come back to Lockwood?" he asked.

"No. It's just that everything is new and I have much to learn. I am the secretary to the Director of Outreach."

After a pause he said, "I am not surprised. I am sure that is a huge responsibility."

"The Red Cross does such wonderful work; it is a constant challenge. I wear a uniform, Alex. It is a gray dress with a broad collar, a white duck hat with yellow braid and white shoes. Can you picture me? It is almost like being in the military."

Another pause before he spoke. "You sound quite settled."

"I'm not that pleased with the rooming house, but I have met another girl here and we get along fine. I will ask you right now before I forget. I would like to come out to Lockwood for a couple of days at Christmas and bring Fannie, that my friend's name."

There was no hesitation. "We would love to have you come. If she is a friend of yours, she is welcome, also. I will have Ella prepare two rooms on the second floor."

A room upstairs? No! Her bedroom and sitting room are right next to the office on the first floor. What had changed? Addie was forthright. "Is my old room not available?"

He cleared his throat. "I have allowed Ella to use it in your absence. It is larger than hers off the kitchen."

The news did not set well. She swallowed her disappointment. "However you want to arrange it is fine," she replied.

"Do you know when you will be coming?"

"No. I will call you next week. Goodbye Alex."

She didn't wait to hear him say goodbye. Addie hung up the receiver and felt the tears welling up. The thought of going to Lockwood for Christmas had lost its excitement. Ella was using her room.

She went to the kitchen and brewed a cup of tea.

When Fannie came home from her day of cleaning at the opulent house she cleaned twice a week, Addie told her that she had talked to Alex and he was agreeable to them visiting at Christmas.

Fannie let out a shout. "Wahoo! I can hardly wait!"

"Alex is letting Ella use my bedroom. What do you think of that? He said he will have her prepare two rooms upstairs."

"What's the matter with that?" asked Fannie.

"It's my room and he is allowing the maid to use it! That's what's the matter with that!"

Fannie lay down on her cot. "I wouldn't get all huffy about it. It's his house and you moved out."

"But I left some personal items for when I visit."

"Is the maid the kind that will lift them?" asked Fannie.

"No she isn't and that's not what bothers me. It's the idea that Alex gave up my room."

271

Fannie got to sitting position on the edge of the bed. "Get over it, Addie. Maybe the one upstairs is nicer."

Addie sat cupping her chin. "I don't know. The only room I went into upstairs belongs to Alex."

Fannie raised an eyebrow. "And?"

"And what?"

"What were you doing in the boss's room?"

"Don't call him the boss. You sound like Jess. It's a long story. I slept in Alex's bed without him in it. Does that answer your lascivious insinuation?" Addie was piqued.

Fannie laughed. "Wow, those are two big words. Let's go have some fish and chips. It will get you out of your funky mood."

Addie smiled and threw a pillow at Fannie. "No Irish Ale! If we're going to Lockwood we have to make plans. This will be our last meal out because we'll have to pinch pennies."

"Let me get up to the ice house I call a room and get a change of clothes. You bring that pad you scribble on and we'll make plans while we sit in the pub."

The pub was noisier than the first time they went. There was a group of men at the bar and they watched as Fannie and Addie walked in.

"Well, if it ain't Fannie Quain and that smart-lookin' gal followin' her," hollered the one called Eddie.

"Yeah," hollered someone else. "Introduce us, Fannie."

Fannie hollered back, "I just saw your wife and four kids, Shanahan. They said it was time for you to stagger home."

This brought a round of raucous laughter and cat calls from the rest before they turned back to the booze-laden bar.

Lucy, the overtaxed waitress, came to take their order. She nodded toward the bar. "They're loud tonight. There'll be a fight before they're done."

Fannie saw Addie's eyes open wide. "That won't happen until after we leave. They're not drunk enough yet."

Addie looked around the crowded, smoky room. What was she doing in this place? It was then she realized how Fannie had grown up. She hadn't had a big farm and the freedom to roam as she pleased. This part of the city was a small town of its own where everyone was familiar; a poorer area with apartment houses, noisy neighbors, drunks in the alley and no place to go. No wonder Fannie wanted to leave. But, she had learned to care for herself and how to meet life head-on.

CHAPTER 38

Christmas would be on a Tuesday so Addie decided the best time for them to go to Lockwood would be on Friday evening on the twenty-first. They could spend all day Saturday and part of Sunday on the farm. As she and Fannie had to report to work on Wednesday, they would have to spend the day of Christmas in Washington. The arrangement was agreeable.

Addie called Alex once the plans were final. Another reverse the charges, wait for permission, and then she heard his voice.

"Hello Adelaide." How formal could he be?

"Hi Alex, it's good to hear your voice. I wanted to tell you that Fannie and I will be coming on Friday, the twenty-first. We have cleared it with our supervisors to leave work at three o'clock." He didn't have to know Fannie's supervisor owned a café. "We will catch the three-thirty train to Bluemont and are expected to arrive there at five-forty."

Alex thought for a moment. "It will be dark by then. I believe it will be best for you to ride into town with Mr. Marks. Someone will pick you up in town and bring you out to the farm."

Someone? She did not detect a note of enthusiasm in his reply.

"Would you prefer that we take a morning train?"

"No. Friday night is fine." His tone was flat.

Addie had a second thought. "Maybe we shouldn't come."

"Certainly you should. Your rooms are ready and I have told the others that you will be coming."

"Then I will see you on the twenty-first. Goodbye Alex."

Addie was bewildered when she hung up the phone. What could be the reason that he sounded so distant? On a farm there are many things that can go awry. He would tell her if there was concern with Lottie or Clay. He would also tell her if it meant a problem with Caleb, Jess or Ella.

After tossing it about in her mind, she had an uneasy feeling that the trouble lay with Alex, himself. What could possibly be wrong? She had ten days before she and Fannie were to make their visit. Until then, her mind would not be settled.

**

Friday afternoon on the twenty-first of December in 1917 Addie and Fannie were waiting for the three-thirty train to take them to the country seventy miles away from the city. When the conductor sounded the "all aboard" the two young women hurried to the railcar and found seats in the front.

"I'm excited as I can be," said Fannie. "This is my first train ride and I can't wait 'til we get to Lockwood."

"Try to relax because we still have over two hours ahead of us," cautioned Addie.

"I know, but don't you just feel like a firefly in a bottle, hopping around and flickering everywhere?"

"I can't say as I do," responded Addie.

"You've got a worry on your mind, I can tell. Afraid the boss man doesn't want us to come?"

Addie looked straight at her. "Will you please stop calling him that? His name is Alex. You sound like you're back in the slave days."

Fannie laughed. "I am a slave… to the café and that big house I have to clean. They pay me slave wages."

Addie couldn't help but laugh. "When we get to Leesburg, it's about half-way. They have a fifteen-minute stop for toilets and refreshments."

"Good. These uncomfortable seats cramp my legs."

By the time they reached the Bluemont station, it was dark outside. The place was lit by a couple of light bulbs hanging from the ceiling and a pot-bellied stove warmed the interior.

They waited in the small room until the stork-like Herbert Marks arrived with a big car to drive them into Berryville. Those taking the car followed a boy who worked at the station and carried a lit lantern. "Got to watch the stones," he advised. "They can trip you up."

At that moment Fannie tripped and caught Addie's arm. "Mother of Saints," she exclaimed. "That was a close one."

There was not a sound from the other three passengers who would ride into town with them.

Fannie whispered to Addie. "Stodgy bunch, aren't they?"

Addie rolled her eyes. What were those at Lockwood going to think of her new-found friend?

They arrived on the corner of the Bank of Clarke County across from the hotel. Herbert Marks unloaded their two suitcases and placed them on the sidewalk. Addie paid the fare. Herbert climbed back into the long auto to take the other passengers farther up the pike.

As she bent to pick up her suitcase, two strong arms swooped her up and whirled her around. "Welcome home, Addie."

"Jess, put me down. You're embarrassing me."

He set her back on her feet.

Fannie was amused. "I was ready to clobber you with my suitcase," she said to Jess. "You must be the big cowboy Addie has told me about. She didn't say you were as good-looking as you are. But these street lights are dim. Maybe you don't look as good as I think."

Jess let out a hearty laugh.

"Jess, this is my friend, Fannie Quain. Fannie, Jess Edwards."

They nodded and smiled at each other.

"I parked the buggy around the corner. Ella threw in a couple of quilts to ward off the chill." He picked up their suitcases and they followed him to the covered buggy.

He drove up Church Street and over to the main road. The town was quiet except for the clip-clop of the horse in the crisp December air. By the time they reached Lockwood they were a friendly trio.

Ella had supper waiting. she heard the buggy pull to the back of the house and ran out waving her hand. "Miss Addie, I ben waitin' for you."

Jess helped the two women down, and Addie rushed to give Ella a warm hug. "I've missed you," she told the girl.

"You got to come back. It ain't, isn't, the same without you bein' here."

"Ella, this is my friend, Miss Fannie."

"Hi, Ella. You're as pretty as Snow White. You can call me Fannie."

"No ma'am. That wouldn't be right. I got supper ready on the stove and the dinin' room set. Mr. Alex said I am suppose' to show you to your rooms an' there's warm water in the bowls, if you want to freshen up."

Addie felt like a visitor and she had only been away for six weeks.

They followed Ella up the stairs where they went into Fannie's room first. For once Fannie was speechless. There was a warm fire in the stone fireplace, a fancy green coverlet with pillows to match on the ornate mahogany bed, a beige upholstered settee and a mahogany dry sink. The high-ceilinged room had been freshly painted and the woodwork shown with a high polish. A braided green rug lay on the wood floor.

Fannie let out a low whistle. "I think I'll stay here forever."

"I'll come get you in fifteen minutes," said Addie. "Ella, you may go back and ready whatever you need for supper."

Addie's room was across the hall from Fannie's. She pushed the door all the way open and drew in her breath. Her favorite color was blue and a warm feeling came over her when she stepped inside. The room had been painted in a restful blue. A satin dark blue bedspread with matching pillows covered a four-poster cherry bed. Two flowered chintz covered chairs sat in front of the red brick fireplace. There was a cherry writing desk and a dresser with a mirror. A wool rug with a medallion in the center lay on the wood floor. She had only peeked into these rooms once before when they were dingy, cold and bare. The transformation was to her liking.

Addie placed her suitcase on the floor and washed her hands before she hurried down the stairs to find Alex. He was in the office hunched over some papers. The door was partially open so she rapped lightly before she stepped in. He looked up when she entered.

"Hello, Alex."

"Hello, Adelaide."

He put down the pencil, leaned back in the chair and looked at her for a long minute. "I'm wrestling with the lineage of these animals," he said. "I want to be sure I have them properly documented."

There was no sign he was happy to see her. His aloofness was disturbing.

"I told Fannie I would bring her for supper in ten minutes."

"She's the friend you've brought with you?" he asked, knowing it wasn't anyone else.

"I want to thank you for letting us come. We both needed a break from the city. You will join us at the table, won't you?"

"Of course. I want to meet your friend."

"Ten minutes," she repeated and turned to leave.

"Addie," Alex said.

She turned back to look at him.

The warmth was back in his brown eyes and a genuine smile creased his angular face. "I'm glad to see you."

She returned his smile and went to get Fannie.

CHAPTER 39

The next morning Lottie greeted them at the door where Addie gave Lottie a big hug before she introduced Fannie.

"Come in from the chill," invited Lottie.

They stepped into the cozy, homey house. The Christmas tree was decorated and the smell of freshly baked gingerbread filled their senses.

"Lottie, you do know how to make a house a home," complimented Addie. "I see you have blossomed," she observed.

"I get tired," admitted Lottie. "But, I feel good and everything is going well. The farm isn't as busy this time of year so Caleb is around more and he's a big help."

"A husband who's a help?" asked Fannie. "Most of the married men I know go to work, go to the bar and let the women do all the work."

"Caleb's not like that," said Addie. "He's a good man." She turned to Lottie. "You might not believe this but I've gone into a bar. They call it a pub, but it's a bar."

Lottie flinched. "That's not like you."

"They have wonderful fish and chips. Fannie knows how to navigate the city and the people in it."

"When we were in Denver," said Lottie, "I thought I would like to live in a city for a while, but once we got back, I know I'm happy to be right where I am."

"You should be," said Fannie. "You've got this comfortable little place you've fixed up and makes others feel welcome the minute they walk in. And outside, it's quiet and you don't have to listen to the trolleys and rattles of delivery trucks or breathe in the smelly air. I could live out here and visit the city twice a year. That would be enough for me. Why did you leave, Addie?"

Addie thought before she replied. She wasn't going to tell Fannie it was because of Alex or that she it was becoming difficult to work side by side without him giving any indication that he cared for her. "I guess I got antsy and needed a change."

Lottie knew exactly why Addie had left. She wasn't going to give her friend away. "How about some hot cider and molasses cookies while you fill me in on what's been going on since you left?" It was the perfect suggestion.

After they left Lottie's house, they went to the barn. The horses were in their stalls and peeking over the half-doors.

"Do you ride these big things?" asked Fannie.

"Sometimes," answered Addie. "Alex is getting a good breeding line going. He's got others, not as good bloodlines as these, he'll sell to the government."

Jess came out of a stall. "Morning gals." He touched his tall hat.

They jumped. "I didn't know you were in here," said Addie.

"I was hauling in some straw from around the corner. What do you think of these beauties, Fannie?"

"I think it's good they're locked up."

He laughed. "You come back in the spring and I'll teach you how to ride one of them. You'd look good on a horse."

That remark pleased Fannie and caused Addie to raise an eyebrow.

"I'm going to take her to see the cattle Alex is breeding," Addie told him.

"We're keeping them penned close to the barn for the winter months. Looks like they're all carrying calves. That should make the boss happy."

Fannie laughed. "Be careful or Addie will jump down your throat for calling him boss."

Jess winked at Fannie. "That's because she's more refined."

"All right you two, you've had your fun. Come on Fannie, I'll show you what Alex is banking his future on."

Caleb was coming into the barn as the women were leaving.

The lean, lanky foreman gave Addie a warm greeting. She introduced Fannie and the two women left for the cattle pen.

Caleb said to Jess, "Addie's friend looks like a lively one."

"She looks like someone I plan on getting to know better," replied Jess.

That evening Lottie invited everyone to their house for an early Christmas dinner. Ella, Addie and Fannie helped her prepare. They borrowed some dishes from the big house. Lottie had made napkins from the Christmas material Leopold Goldman had given her. They looked festive on the white muslin tablecloth.

Fannie made a pumpkin brandy pie. Addie knew Alex kept spirits in a cupboard so she and Fannie poured out a fourth of a cup of brandy to put in the pie. "This isn't going to affect us, is it?" she asked Fannie.

"Not a bit," Fannie assured her. "It will give the pie some flavor."

Alex was invited and he agreed to come. "It would be impolite not to accept the invitation," he said.

That evening the Dunn house was crowded with seven people squeezed around the kitchen table. They had roast chicken, potatoes, gravy, biscuits, baked squash and green beans followed by the brandied pumpkin pie. Lottie brought gingerbread cookies to the table.

Fannie had never had hard cider. Caleb had made some and said it was his version of nog. After a few swallows Fannie announced it went down easier than Irish whiskey, which brought questionable looks from those present.

Jess and Caleb brought out their guitars and entertained with western songs. When they played a fast tune Fannie got up and showed how to dance an Irish jig. Either brandy in the pie, or the hard cider, or both caused her to be tipsy, and she fell into Alex's lap.

"Whoops!" she exclaimed. "That cider of yours has got a kick, Caleb."

Addie sucked in her breath.

Jess was quick to take Fannie's hand and raise her to her feet.

"A fancy jig it is," said Alex. "I believe we've had enough revelry for one night," he said.

Fannie looked at him and said, "You know, boss. You're not such a bad egg."

Addie wanted to drop through the floor.

They put on their coats and headed for the big house after thanking Caleb and Lottie for a delightful evening. Ella had left when the meal was over and dishes cleaned up.

Jess walked out the door with them. "You gals come to my cabin in the morning and I'll make breakfast."

Fannie waved her arm in his direction. "I wouldn't miss it!"

**

The next morning Addie and Fannie were in Jess's cabin eating breakfast. He fixed bacon, scrambled eggs and biscuits. The coffee was strong so Addie added milk to hers.

"I need that to clear my head," said Fannie of the coffee. "That hard cider has a kick. I didn't make too much of a fool of myself, I hope."

"You were fine," Jess assured her. "Addie said you were born and raised in the city."

"City girl from the day I landed."

"I was a city boy, too," he told her. "I gave it up for country life. I'd go back to visit but I wouldn't want to live there."

"I didn't know you lived in a city," said Addie.

Jess inclined his head toward her. "I keep telling you there's a lot you don't know about me."

Addie switched the subject. "Jess refinished the table and chairs, Fannie."

Fannie ran her hand over the smoothness of the wood. "Didn't you also sketch that picture of the farm Addie has?"

"Guilty," he replied.

Fannie cupped her chin in her hands and batted her expressive green eyes at him. "You would be a handy man to have around."

"I've tried to convince people of that," he answered looking over at Addie.

"It wouldn't take long to convince me," Fannie said.

Addie's jaw dropped.

"How would it be if I made a visit down to Washington and take you gals out for an evening on the town?" he said.

Fannie clapped her hands. "Anytime you feel like it. We'll be waiting."

When they left his cabin Addie admonished Fannie. "Did you have to be so flirty with Jess? I can't imagine what he thinks."

With a toss of her red head, Fannie replied. "He probably thinks I'd be fun on a date. You've got to learn to unbend, Addie."

"I don't want to unbend too much. I was mortified when you fell on Alex last evening."

Fannie was remorseful. "Yeah, I did feel bad about that. Once you get past his stuffiness, he's all right."

"He's not stuffy," Addie defended him.

"All I can say is that if you would bend a little this way and he would bend a little that way, you may be surprised at what happens. I've seen the way he looks at you."

"Alex is close to forty years old," replied Addie.

"What difference does that make? I've seen plenty of men marry younger women and they make good husbands. They're settled and got all the brashness out of them."

Addie chuckled. "What makes you such a wise woman at eighteen?"

"I had to grow up when I was ten and I paid close attention to what was going on around me," Fannie answered.

Addie checked the watch pin Clay had given her. "We need to pack up because we have to be up on the mountain in an hour. Alex said he will drive us to Bluemont."

"Wahoo!" exclaimed Fannie. "I get to ride in that fancy car of his."

Fannie went to her room to pack and Addie went to the office where Alex was working.

"We'll be ready to go in about fifteen minutes," she told him.

He sat back in his chair. "I'm not sure your new friend is a good influence on you."

"Fannie has had a different road to travel than I've had. She may seem unrefined around the edges, but she is a good soul. She has taught me much."

Alex shrugged a shoulder.

Addie was miffed. "She said you need to unbend. Maybe she is right. We'll be down in a few minutes if you still want to drive us to the train!"

"Why do we seem to chafe each other, Addie?" he asked.

She heaved a heavy sigh. "I don't know. I don't want to leave on an unhappy note. We have had a great time. Thank you for letting us come."

He left the desk chair and came to where she stood. He took her hand in his. "You are not a visitor. You will always be a part of this place." He brought her fingers to his lips. "You had better go and pack."

Alex took the back road to the main road and on up the mountain.

Fannie jabbered away at what a wonderful time she'd had this weekend. Addie was quiet but Fannie was never at a loss for words.

Alex carried their cases into the station. Before he turned to leave he addressed Fannie, "It was a pleasure to have you visit."

"Thank you, Alex." she replied. "It was the most enjoyable time I have ever had, and it was kind of you to allow me to come." She went to sit in a corner of the room where she struck up a conversation with another passenger waiting for the train.

Alex took Addie's hand. "I wish you would stay."

"I can't," she replied.

"Call me to let me know you arrived safely."

Addie nodded because the tears were about to spill.

He went out the door and she wanted to run after him. Instead, she swallowed hard and went to sit next to Fannie.

"Are you all right?' Fannie asked.

Addie took a deep breath. "I am. You were gracious to Alex," she said.

Fannie struck a haughty pose. "I can be diplomatic when I have to be."

Addie smiled. "I think it will be good to get back to work."

CHAPTER 40

In Washington the stores were decorated for Christmas. Addie didn't feel in the Christmas mood. Monday she went to work and hoped that would perk up her spirits, but the mood persisted.

On Tuesday, Christmas day, Fannie went to be with her family. Although Addie was invited she declined because she didn't feel well. She had a headache and her joints ached. The damp, cold air in Washington seemed to penetrate to the bone. Addie stayed at the apartment all of Christmas day. She drank hot tea and put a Vicks poultice on her chest.

She reread Clay's letters and tried to get Alex off her mind. Perhaps it wasn't such a good idea to have gone back to the farm. She thought about Clay and wondered how he was spending the holiday. Did he feel as forlorn as she felt?

The phone in the hall rang and she went to answer it. It would be for either her or Fannie because the other three women, who seemed to live in their own worlds, never used the phone. Icy Eleanor had her own private line.

"Hello."

"Hello, Addie. It's Alex. I wanted to wish you a Merry Christmas."

The sound of his voice boosted her despondent feelings. "It is so good of you to call," she said.

"You sound stuffy."

"I'm coming down with a cold, but I am drinking tea, doctoring with Vicks and resting. Fannie has gone to spend the day with her parents."

"You shouldn't be alone on Christmas."

"It is my choice. Fannie asked me to go with her. I just didn't feel up to it. What are your plans for the day?"

He tried to sound upbeat. "Ella has gone to be with her family. I will be staying here. Lottie invited Jess and me for dinner."

Addie wished she could be right there with them. "You will be well fed."

There was concern in his voice. "I know you need your rest so I don't want to keep you on the phone. If you get sick you are to have Fannie call me right away."

"It is a cold, Alex. I'll feel better in a couple of days. I have to go into work tomorrow, that's the reason I decided to stay in and rest today."

He agreed it was a good decision. "This weather isn't the best. I feel a bit out of sorts myself."

"Tea, Vicks, and rest and you'll feel like a new man."

He laughed. "Merry Christmas, Adelaide."

"Merry Christmas, Alex."

Fannie came back to the apartment around six o'clock in the evening. "I brought you some ham and potatoes and bean soup. Do you feel better?"

"Is that a new scarf?" asked Addie.

Fannie smiled. "A Christmas present that my mom knitted for me."

"It's lovely. That took a lot of work to weave the different shades of green."

"My mother is good with her hands." She threw a bag at Adelaide. "She knitted one for you, too."

Addie pulled the wool scarf, knitted with strands of navy, red and white, out of the paper bag. She wrapped it around her neck and flared out her arms. "How do I look?"

"Like you need a week's rest," replied Fannie.

"Oh, do I look that bad? I've been coughing and sneezing all day. Maybe you shouldn't sleep in this room. You might catch it."

"Whatever it is, I've probably already caught it, and I am not about to sleep up in the ice house. I will have to bring down my clothes for work tomorrow. Want me to heat up some bean soup for you?" asked a caring Fannie.

"I would love to have some," answered Adelaide. "Alex called to wish me a Merry Christmas."

"Saints be!" declared her friend. "Next, he'll be asking you to marry him."

"That's a far cry from a telephone call. He's never even kissed me or shown any signs that he cares for me, if he does."

Fannie sat in the chair across from Addie. "How blind can you be? I spent two days up there and I know how he feels about you. His problem is that he hesitates because he's older than you. Your problem is that you are afraid to make the first move."

"You've got it all figured out," scoffed Addie.

"All I had to do was open my eyes. Jess, on the other hand, is a different story."

Addie sent a wry look in her friend's direction. "You've figured out Alex but you can't figure Jess? You flirted with him enough."

"You bet I did. He thinks he's got a soft spot for you, too, but I plan on changing his mind." Fannie laughed. "He's going to take us out for a night on the town so you had better not be ailing because I'm planning on New Year's Eve."

"He didn't say that."

"You watch. I gave him the telephone number here."

Addie shook her head. "You aren't shy, Fannie Quain. I don't know how he's going to call you because the only phone on the farm is in the office. It is not for use by the farmhands."

"See? There you are getting all stiff-necked again. You just wait and see. I've set my cap for that big, good-lookin' cowboy."

"You only just met him."

"I've seen enough men I can size them up pretty fast. My mother said, 'Fannie, if you want something go after it because it sure ain't comin' to you.' Jess is just what I want."

Fannie went to the kitchen and heated up the bean soup for Addie. Then she retrieved her frigid clothes from her attic room.

"I do feel better after the warm soup," said Addie.

"Good," replied Fannie. "I brought down the Irish whiskey and you're having a shot before you go to bed whether you want one or not."

"Do you ever worry that you might turn into a lush?" asked Addie.

Fannie shook her head. "No. I'm happy with my life. It's when you let the world get you down that the problems begin."

Addie sighed. "I wish I had your outlook."

Fannie thought for a minute. "When I get up in the morning I decide whether to be happy or sad, and I choose the happy side. Too often people let the cares of the day wear at them. That's easy to do. The future is unsure so I enjoy every little moment that comes along."

Addie coughed and blew her nose.

"You had better hop into your nightclothes and have that shot so you can get a good sleep," advised Fannie. "And, don't get any sicker because we have to find some fancy duds for New Year's Eve."

"You're impossible," said Addie.

CHAPTER 41

Addie went to work Wednesday, Thursday and Friday. She was worn out. When she looked in the mirror dark circles under eyes and a tired, pale face stared back at her. Her chest hurt from coughing.

Fannie was healthy and helped as much as she could. She tried to convince Addie to stay home from work, but Addie insisted she needed the money and they needed her at work.

"They won't need you if you're dead," Fannie remarked.

Addie planned on resting the whole weekend. Fannie had to work for a few hours on Saturday but assured Addie she would stay around the apartment after work.

Jess hadn't called to take her out on New Year's Eve but Fannie had bought a fancy dress of jade green satin. The fitted dress hugged every curve of her shapely body.

"You're not going out in that dress without a chaperone, I hope," said Addie.

"No, Jess will be my bodyguard."

"Fannie, he hasn't called. You should have saved your money."

The phone in the hall rang. "That should be Alex," said a nonchalant Fannie.

"Alex?"

"Yes, I called him and told him he should come because you are wearing yourself out," Fannie answered.

Addie tried to get up out of bed, but it was too much effort. She lay her head back on the pillow. "You shouldn't have done that!" was her admonishment. But Fannie was out the door and answering the phone. Addie could hear muffled voices without understanding what was said.

She came back into the room. "Alex said you should have gone to see a doctor."

"What else did he say?"

"He said he'll handle it."

"What did he mean by that? He's seventy miles away."

"I didn't ask," said Fannie, "I just relayed the information. I'm fixing you some tea and hot cereal. Then you need to sleep."

Addie was too weary to argue. When Fannie brought the tea, Addie drank it, but she only ate a taste of the Cream of Rice cereal. "I'm sorry Fannie. I have no appetite."

"I have to work over at the mansion for a couple of hours. Is there anything you need before I go?" asked Fannie.

"Just some rest," Addie replied.

**

The next day Addie heard commotion in the downstairs hall. She heard the disgruntled voice of Eleanor Hopkins and that of a male. From the high-pitch of Eleanor's voice, Addie knew it was serious. Weak and wobbly, she got out of bed and unlocked the door to try to hear what was going on.

She recognized Alex's voice. "I am here to see Miss Richards. She is ill."

"Men can't come in this house!"

"I am a lawyer. If necessary, I will go to the police and secure a warrant."

Eleanor was quiet. She regained what dignity she could muster and said, "That will not be necessary. You have ten minutes. She's upstairs. The room number is three."

Addie was in her nightclothes so she made her way back to bed.

He rapped before opening the door, which was ajar. "My God, it is stifling in here!"

"What are you doing here, Alex?"

"That's a fine greeting," he said.

"I'm sorry. I don't feel up to company."

Alex came and sat on the side of the bed. "Fannie said you were sick. I came to take you home, Addie."

"Home?"

"Home to Lockwood. You belong there with me. I've been a fool."

Addie smiled at him. "That's what Jess said." She saw the warmth in his brown eyes, his hair neatly combed, and his clean shaven face. She raised a hand and placed it on the side of his cheek.

"Are you sure?" she asked.

Millie Curtis

He took her hand in his. "I was not pleased when you left. I wrestled with myself. I couldn't tell you my feelings because I didn't think our age difference was fair to you. Then I thought about Clay. I know he cares for you and I felt guilty harboring my feelings for you. When Fannie called, panic gripped me and the guilt flew. I am sure and became surer every anxious mile of the way here. Addie, with all my faults I'm asking you to marry me."

Her response was without hesitation. "It has taken you long enough. Oh, Alex, of course I will! Now I'm sick and you can't even kiss me, which I have longed for ever since the evening we spent in the Tabor Opera House in Leadville."

He kissed the fingers of the hand he held. "You have been in my mind since the day Clay introduced us at the stables. But it was in Leadville when you started muddling my thoughts."

"You have been slow at bringing your feelings to life. If you had shown any inclination of caring for me, I wouldn't have left."

He stroked her face with his finger. "If you meant to teach me a lesson, you have succeeded. I'll make up for it."

They heard the ringing of a bell. "I believe that is your landlady telling me my ten minutes are up."

"When will you come back?"

"I'm staying at the Willard and I have a room reserved for you. When Fannie called I told her I would take care of things."

A weak smile came to Addie. "Poor Fannie. She was sure Jess would take her out on the town on New Year's Eve."

"Oh, he will. When he heard I was coming, he rode into the city with me. Said he promised you gals a night on the town. I told him you would not be one of the 'gals'. I believe it will take a man like Jess to corral your friend."

"Fannie has been good for me."

The bell rang in earnest.

"I have to leave." He gave her a gentle kiss on the forehead. "I will be here at nine o'clock in the morning to take you to the hotel."

"Alex, tomorrow is the last day of the year. I have to work. I can't quit on a day's notice."

He pulled her into his strong arms. "Why not? Think about it, Addie. Tomorrow night is New Year's Eve. We can spend a quiet evening and be on our way to Lockwood the next day with a new year ahead of us."

They heard Eleanor Hopkins stomping up the stairs.

He kissed her cheek. "Tomorrow morning at nine."

Addie heard Alex apologize to Eleanor in his soothing voice when he closed the door. Whatever else he said was lost to her ears.

She lay back on her pillow reliving the past few moments. Alex had asked her to marry him. Nothing else mattered. She would hand in her resignation tomorrow morning.

Fannie was coming up the stairs when the phone rang so she answered it before going into Addie's room. After hanging up the receiver she danced into the room. "Guess who's going to spend New Year's Eve with her special cowboy?"

Addie gave a twisted smile. "Guess who's going to marry Alex Lockwood?"

Fannie's jaw dropped. "You're not delirious are you?"

Addie sat up and clasped her hands around her knees. "He came by a while ago. I still can't believe it. He said Jess rode in with him. You were right, Fannie. He'll be your bodyguard for New Year's Eve."

Fannie flipped her red hair. "I know my men," she replied.

Addie moved to sit on the side of the bed. "If you hadn't called Alex to tell him I was sick, none of this would have happened."

Fannie sat in a chair. "Do you ever wonder if it was Providence that brought us together? My mother says the Lord has his ways. Your unhappiness drove you to leave and I was not so politely told to leave my house. Then we both end up in this gloomy rooming house."

"I'm leaving in the morning," Addie informed. "I will hand in my resignation, and Alex and I will head back to Lockwood the next day. You can take over this apartment and get out of the attic. I had to pay for six months so it is paid up for four more months."

Fannie left the chair and hugged her friend. "You are a peach, Adelaide Richards. Maybe I'll have my feet on the ground by then."

Addie smiled at her wise young friend. "Who knows?"

CHAPTER 42

Addie felt better the next day. She was up early and packed her belongings to wait for Alex. He arrived promptly at nine o'clock. Eleanor Hopkins allowed him to come to the room to get Addie's things. The landlady was satisfied to let Fannie stay in Addie's apartment as long as Fannie still paid the attic rent for four more months. Fannie agreed as Addie's room was paid for and it was nice to have a warm bed.

Alex drove Addie to Walter Reed Army Hospital where her Red Cross supervisor was not pleased with Addie's resignation, but he was understanding. The Great War was causing uncertainty in the country and people were getting used to daily changes in their lives, trying to find happiness where they could.

They arrived at the Willard around noon. Addie rested most of the day in her room in the hotel. She sat by the window enjoying the luxury of being able to look out onto the Washington scene after living in the windowless room at the townhouse.

Alex had an appointment with a government official. He explained to Addie that he made the appointment when he knew he would be in the city. It's like killing two birds with one stone is the way he put it. Addie wasn't pleased with his choice of words.

They ate dinner in her room. Alex had steak and Addie ordered potato soup. Her stomach had not returned to the point of heavy food.

Later in the evening she felt well enough to go to the dining room with Alex, which was gaily decorated for a New Year's Eve celebration. Alex smiled over at her as they sat at a table covered with a white linen tablecloth and a glowing candle. Damask napkins of red and green design made her think of Leadville and the evenings she, Lottie and Anna Tygert had spent sewing Christmas napkins.

How could a way of life change so much in two years? Now she was sitting across from the man she was going to marry and begin a new journey.

At midnight the bells in the churches rang out, bands played, horns tooted. People were wrapped in each other's arms and kissing under the mistletoe.

Alex came to Addie's side. "This must be done properly," he said. He went down on one knee beside her, took her left hand in his and placed a sparkling ring on her finger. "Adelaide Richards, you are the woman I love. Will you marry me?"

Addie smiled back at the man she adored. "I gave you my answer yesterday and I haven't changed my mind." She placed her hands on each side of his face and kissed him squarely on the lips. "I don't care if you catch my cold or not. We'll go home to Lockwood and recover together."

Alex laughed, stood, and pulled her to her feet. "We're together in everything from now on?"

Addie admired the diamond ring on her finger. "I promise."

He kissed her once again. "I love you, Adelaide Richards. Do you know what you have said yes to?"

Of course she knew!

About the Author

This sixth novel by Mille Curtis is set in Clarke County, Virginia where she lives with her husband of fifty-eight years. She finds the early 1900's a fascinating time not only for the fashions of the day but also for the ways in which America was changing. Her novels are a bit of history, a bit of humor and a bit of romance.

Other books by Millie Curtis

Beyond the Red Gate
The Milliner
The Newcomer
Window of Hope
Of Course She Knew!

Books available at: www.amazon.com, www.barnesandnoble.com

CPSIA information can be obtained at www.ICGtesting.com
Printed in the USA
BVOW08s0928090916

461112BV00001B/1/P